SIX EARLY STORIES

Thomas Mann

SIX EARLY STORIES

*

Translated from the German with a Note
by Peter Constantine
Edited with an Introduction
by Burton Pike

SUN &
MOON

CLASSICS

109

LOS ANGELES
SUN & MOON PRESS
1997

Sun & Moon Press
A Program of The Contemporary Arts Educational Project, Inc.
a nonprofit corporation
6026 Wilshire Boulevard, Los Angeles, California 90036
http:www.sunmoon.com

First Published by Sun & Moon Press in 1997
10 9 8 7 6 5 4 3 2 1

This book was made possible, in part, through contributions to
The Contemporary Arts Educational Project, Inc., a nonprofit corporation.

Cover: Oskar Schlemmer, *Römisches* (Roman), 1925
Kunstmuseum, Basel
Design: Katie Messborn
Typography: Guy Bennett

LIBRARY OF CONGRESS CATALOGING IN PUBLICATION DATA
Mann, Thomas [1875–1955]
Six Early Stories
p. cm — (Sun & Moon Classics: 109)
ISBN: 1-55713-298-4
I. Title. II. Series. III. Translators
811'.54—dc20

Printed in the United States of America on acid-free paper.

CONTENTS

INTRODUCTION

When *Stories of Three Decades,* containing translations of many of Mann's stories into English, was published in 1936, a number of his early pieces were not included. The translator of that volume, Helen T. Lowe-Porter, wrote in her preface that with the publication of Mann's first collection of stories, *Der kleine Herr Friedemann* (*Little Herr Friedemann*), in 1898, "the youth of twenty after some tentative and awkward efforts entered the literary field." Times and interests change; in 1936 Thomas Mann, in exile from Nazi Germany, was celebrated as a leading spokesman for the threatened humanistic values of Western civilization. His early development as a writer was not on anyone's mind at the time, and Mrs. Lowe-Porter's exclusion of these stories as "tentative and awkward efforts" now seems both arbitrary and wrong. They are very much of a piece with Mann's other early work, and cast an important light on both his early development and the care and skill with which he worked at his craft.

In spite of his often-stated allegiance to the bourgeois tradition, in his ambition and his search for a new style Mann was from the beginning an experimenter and a modernist rather than a writer in the traditional vein. Thanks partly to Mrs. Lowe-Porter's stately translations of his major works into English, and partly also to his own later, self-styled role as spokesman for Western culture, Mann appears to the English-speaking world as a far more traditional kind of writer than he in fact ever was. The stories presented here offer an opportunity to help reassess this picture.

The present collection thus makes available in English the missing initial portion of a major writer's artistic development. It also provides an extraordinary insight into the changes that were taking place on the European literary scene in the 1890s, as the decadence and fatigue of the Fin-de-siècle was giving way to an energetic post-Nietzschean modernism. The whole notion of what constituted realism in fiction was being turned inside out.

Thomas Mann was twenty-five when, in 1901, he achieved instant fame with the publication of his first novel, *Buddenbrooks, Decay of a Family.* He had been writing for some seven years, mostly well-received literary sketches for newspapers and periodicals, chief among them the satirical *Simplicissimus,* of which he was an editor for a time (1898–1900). While *Buddenbrooks* (1901) and *Tonio Kröger* (1902) stand as Mann's most complete early achievements, they obscure the radical experimentation that can be seen more clearly in the stories and sketches that led up to them, notably in those that were left out of *Stories of Three Decades.*

The stories presented here already set out many of Mann's basic themes, which can be traced as far forward in his work as *Doctor Faustus* and *Felix Krull*: among them the doubled central figure of narrator and hero, the nervous states evident in the style as well as the characters, the alienation of a sensitive outsider from bourgeois society but not from bourgeois culture, the ambiguous and problematic role of women, the combination of satire and sharp naturalistic observation with a new kind of psychology of the senses derived largely from Nietzsche.

Nietzsche, one of Thomas Mann's early and enduring idols, first championed this new and destabilizing psychology, sweeping away the notions of a confidently centered self and a confidently centered society. ("The most characteristic quality of modern man," Nietzsche had written in *The Use and Abuse of History for Life*, is "the strange contrast between an inner life to which nothing outward corresponds, and an outward existence unrelated to what is within.")

Philosophers, psychologists, sociologists, and writers rushed into the heady vacuum Nietzsche had opened up. The sociologist Georg Simmel wrote in 1909 that "the essence of modernity as such is psychologism, the experiencing and interpretation of the world in terms of the reactions of our inner life and indeed as an inner world, the dissolution of fixed contents in the fluid element of the soul, from which all that is substantive is filtered and where forms are merely forms of motion." Freud's investigations arose from the intense interest in psychology in the generation preceding his. (Freud came to public attention a little too late to be a formative influence on Mann, although Mann picked up on him a decade or so later.)

Unaware of this background, the modern reader might be tempted to focus exclusively on the conflicted central figures in these stories, and read them as confessional outpourings on the part of their brittle young author. There is some point to this, but while Mann always stylized himself in his writings, there is a good deal more to them. To a far greater extent than the modern reader might realize, Mann's early writings are deliberate experiments on the cutting edge of the literary themes and techniques of the time. Most of them were written for newspapers and magazines, to introduce these new ways to a broad reading public accustomed to conventional fare. That their new approach was praised by contemporary critics was an indication of Mann's success.

These stories show a talented writer of already considerable technical sophistication forming his literary voice from the social and scientific concerns of the day as well as from his own conflicted self. Mann was, and remained, a cool professional (an attitude of his that he was to satirize in Gustav von Aschenbach in *Death in Venice,* and in the figure of the confidence-man Felix Krull). In these early stories we see him testing out the tools of his craft with ideas and techniques that, at the beginning, owed much to the Goncourts, Paul Bourget, Storm, Heine, Nietzsche, and (briefly) to the anti-Naturalist Hermann Bahr. Mann seems to be harking back in these stories to the decadence of Huysman's novel *Against the Grain* (1884) and to the decadent naturalism of Zola's *Nana* (1880), although Mann claimed that he owed a greater debt to the Goncourt brothers than to Huysmans or Zola. But far from being imitations, Mann's experiments form the laboratory bench for a new approach to art. His subject matter is largely an assault on the clichés of nineteenth-century and Fin-de-siècle literature, already faded at the time Mann was writing, but his approach and style are new.

The new psychology that came out of both science and philosophy in the early 1890s saw the self no longer as a single, socially-determined personality, but as a complex and ever-shifting totality of successive moments in time determined by inner forces: physiology, nerves, stimuli, perceptions, consciousness, and feelings. For German and Austrian writers of Mann's generation, including Musil, Rilke, Kafka, and Schnitzler, among others, the self was fragmented and, like society itself, centered not in a notion of wholeness but in an unstable succession of fluid perceptions, sensations, and cognition. In literature, the notion of the self became an experimental field of operations rather than the socially and structurally determined "character" it had been in the earlier, traditional sense. Following Nietzsche, art had become knowledge (*Erkenntnis*), experimental in the sense of contributing to an understanding of the world the way science did. This view, enunciated for instance by

Zola in "The Experimental Novel" (1880), was widespread in the generation that came to maturity around 1900.

Nietzsche, who psychologized everything, also psychologized aesthetics. The world can only be grasped as an aesthetic phenomenon, the young Thomas Mann read in *The Birth of Tragedy*. Nietzsche equated aesthetics and ethics, so that art became a tool for understanding cultural values and morality, a concept that was later to become of central importance for Mann. In these stories we see Mann attempting in various tentative ways to seek a new unity in art that would combine psychology, aesthetics, and ethics.

The structural tension in these pieces typically takes the form of a triangle. On one side is the fixed, ordered, and well-off social world, both middle-class and patrician, a world of physical health, normality, and unquestioned acceptance of prevailing bourgeois values. The second side is occupied by a central character, mentally creative but unstable and physically weak, who is a not-quite-outcast outsider to the social world. The third side of the triangle is taken by the narrator, who is difficult to place. He is seemingly detached and analytical, frequently satirical, and yet at the same time he often throbs with genuinely intense, conflicted feelings—Thomas Mann's famous "irony." The center of these stories seems to lie in the narrator's relation to the characters and situations he presents.

This triangular disposition of elements, which was to

remain a prominent feature of Mann's work, destabilizes these stories. The reader's attention is constantly divided between the other characters, the social situation, and the mercurial narrator. Mann's concern seems to be to dramatize what Harry Liebersohn has called in another context "personal fragmentation within an impersonal order." The impersonal order is imposed on the fragmented central character from one side by the clichés of conservative social mores, and from the other by the detached, involved, and skeptical narrator. There are traces of Dostoevsky here, but the destabilization of the world is far more radical than in the Russian writer. The social mores in these stories are satirized and caricatured, and most of the characters and situations are what by Mann's time were the threadbare, rhetorically melodramatic literary devices familiar in nineteenth-century fiction, especially French: A sensitive well-to-do young man falling in love with an actress, or a proper, rich family refusing to accept an artist as a son-in-law, were clichés already for Balzac.

This satiric assault was deliberate. Mann's interest this early in his career was not in the structure of the social or political world as such (even in *Buddenbrooks* this remains subservient to the psychology of character), but in the psychological profiling of a decentered character in a conventional social setting, often a gathering of some kind. The psychological interest in these stories and sketches centers around what Goethe, in referring to a troubled person, called "the disproportion between the talent and the life," an idea that Mann takes over in Nietzschean form, a large talent lodged in a weak body and suffering mind, and that he applies, notably, to the artist or the person of artistic temperament.

This disproportion is central to Mann's efforts to create a detached yet credible narrator who could encompass and relate the situation in a modern manner rather than in the manner of popular fiction. (Again, most of these stories were written for newspapers and magazines.) But the persona of the narrator gives the writer trouble. There seem to be in these pieces powerful, free-floating feelings that resist incorporation into the stories' triangular structures and into the characters. The reader feels a constant struggle between the strongly ambivalent feelings and the form. The feelings seem incommensurate with the conventional values of the social world that is satirized and caricatured, and yet it is a world whose values the narrator cannot bring himself to dismiss out of hand. The social caricatures are prejudices from the stock repertory of patrician European stereotypes of the time, abhorrent as they seem to us (the bejeweled *arriviste* Baron von Stein in *The Will to Happiness*, for instance, or his Jewish wife). At the same time, this brutally caricatured couple is extremely kind to the sickly artist Paolo Hofmann, and they show exquisite parental concern for their daughter.

This ambivalence also finds notable expression in the female characters. The male outsider figures cannot manage to establish a relationship with any of them: The men seem to fear the passionate involvement they seek with the women. The women, however, with the possible exception of Angela in *Anecdote,* are not seen as predatory vampires on the order of Zola's Nana or Wedekind's Lulu, but as ordinary people realistically concerned with leading lives of their own, circumscribed as they are by the unforgiving conventions of their social positions. The enigmatic, self-contained, emancipated woman was to become a Mann "type," on the order of Lisabeta in *Tonio Kröger,* or Claudia Chauchat in *The Magic Mountain.* The conflicted ambivalence of feelings seems to be characteristic not of Mann's women, but of his men, not least of his narrators. Is Angela in *Anecdote* a demon? We see her through the eyes of her husband, who considers her one, and yet the story allows us to glimpse an Angela who might well be the victim of a jealous spouse. In *The Will to Happiness,* the struggling artist Paolo Hofmann, having after many years married the tender woman he loves and who has long loved him, dies almost immediately, on the morning after his wedding night. He had to die, because "once his will to happiness was satisfied he no longer had a pretext to live."

In these early stories, then, Mann was experimenting with a complex, multi-layered narrative. A first- or third-person narrator is involved in a psychological duet with the central character in a social situation. The character is totally caught in the situation; the narrator is the scientific experimenter, the detached observer. Yet there is always an undercurrent indicating the narrator's subtle involvement with the central character or situation. The realistic external descriptions are often ironic (in *Fallen* we read: "And then he mutely kissed her picture and put on a clean shirt and his good suit and shaved the stubble on his chin and went to the Heustrasse"). The characters, settings, and action of these stories are deliberately trivialized in order to focus attention on the feelings and sensations of the "outsider" character and the narrator—not on their actions. These characters have lots of problems with their feelings; when it comes to action, they are are tongue-tied and inhibited, especially in sexual matters.

The first-person pieces, *A Vision, Death,* and *Avenged,* offer an interesting insight into Mann's experimentation with technique. The narrator of *A Vision* is clearly detached, speaking in his own person as an "inside outsider," trying to analyze dispassionately his *own* hallucinatory sensation of a lost love. The break at the very end of this story suddenly snaps the reader back to the sentimental "love story" of popular romantic fiction, perhaps to emphasize how far Mann's new psychological-analytical way of writing is from the traditional expectations of the popular press of the day. *Death* seems to be a story about a situation only, and for an odd reason: it was an entry in a competition run by the magazine *Simplicissimus* for a story in which "sexual love plays no role." (Another writer, Jakob Wassermann, won first prize, but the periodical printed Mann's story as well.)

In *Avenged,* Mann tries combining the first-person narrator with the central character who is telling a social gathering the story of an earlier romantic involvement. The separation in time between present and past allows Mann to bring into the story the ironizing element of analytic distance from the emotion he is recalling.

These stories, then, are especially interesting as the experiments of an ambitious and coolly professional craftsman intent on developing a new, post-Nietzschean, psychological style. They present ambivalent psychology and feelings, but they are nothing like the confessional outpourings of a disturbed soul. A short time later Mann was to develop in his fiction an astonishing variety of tonal registers, displaying in the original German an astounding technical virtuosity that differs markedly from work to work and even within a work, as happens in *Tonio Kröger* and *Death in Venice.* Allowing for the differences, Oscar Wilde's *The Picture of Dorian Gray,* with its subversive and virtuosic tonal registers, is perhaps the closest analog in English to the effects Mann was reaching for here. These differing stylistic registers are one aspect of the mimicry that Mann himself called attention to as an essential feature of his art. Mimicry is an act of appropriation, of disguise, of borrowed plumage; it differs from direct representation in the irony, the conscious awareness of difference, of distance, between style and subject. In these stories we see the young writer's often extravagant attempts to manipulate this complex ironic style so that serious meaning resonates through both the narrator's critical observations and the sharp social satire. This was a task of formidable difficulty for the beginning writer, but clearly audible is the strong, fresh voice of a major talent.

The translations are based on Mann's *Gesammelte Werke in Zwölf Bänden* (Frankfurt: S. Fischer Verlag, 1960), Vol. VIII. For some of the information in the Introduction and headnotes I would like to acknowledge my debt to Hans Rudolf Vaget's valuable *Thomas Mann: Kommentar zu sämtlichen Erzählungen* (Munich, 1984).

—BURTON PIKE

TRANSLATOR'S NOTE

One of the most interesting challenges in translating these early stories of Thomas Mann has been to capture his subtle shifts in language and his idiosyncratic and volatile tone. One might mistakenly perceive these stylistic incongruities as the weakness of a young writer struggling to find his voice.

When I first stumbled onto these stories I was struck by how different Mann's early use of language was compared to the language of his later work. I was surprised to find that these stories had never appared in English, although *Vision* had been translated into Japanese.

As these six pieces show, it is extraordinary how linguistically rebellious Thomas Mann was in his teens and early twenties, especially in relation to Naturalism and Aestheticism. In these stories we see him vigorously subverting the literary trends of the 1890s by using the language and themes of the time against the grain.

In his first published story, *Vision*, we get a strong foretaste of the exotic blending of levels of diction that characterizes these early works. The opening sentence with its sparse punctuation draws the reader in with its rhythm:

As I mechanically roll another cigarette and the speckles of brown dust tumble onto the yellow-white blotting paper of my writing folder....

But as the protagonist is gripped by the "vision," Mann shifts to impressionistic sentences that are quite radical and unusual for the time. He first slips into slang — "Now the silence has gone to the dogs" (*Aber nun ist die Ruhe zum Teufel*) — and then continues with abrupt, staccato phrases and almost Expressionist syntax:

Jangling movement in all my senses. Feverish, nervous, crazed. Every sound stabs!

Mann's experiments in diction become even more striking in the following stories. Especially interesting is his use of vernacular, even slang expressions, to color the speech of his characters. Rölling, for example, a boisterously cynical medical student in *Fallen,* is characterized throughout the story by his lively, fast-paced speech:

'I saw the two of you last night!' Rölling said one day. 'My respects! No one has ever managed to get this far with her. Good job!... She must be head over heels in love with you! You should just go for it!'

In *The Will to Happiness* Mann is even more iconoclastic. He puts the rough-and-tumble vernacular of his generation into the mouth of the smitten romantic hero. The first words we hear this young artist utter in response to the narrator's query whether he intends to settle down in Munich are:

> Well, why not? I like the city; I like it a lot. The whole tone, you know. The people, too! And what's also important, a painter's social position here is superb, even an unknown painter's. There's nowhere better...."

What perhaps makes reading these stories most interesting is the rhythm of the writing, with tones that change and shift—at times from one paragraph to the next. We see Mann forging his characters, cutting analytically through their psychological makeup with labyrinthine, multi-claused sentences—a trademark of his later work. But often a youthful energy, even impatience, sets in as tension mounts behind the slow, potent, tight-knit language. Readers who enjoy the older Mann's forceful writing, his controlled style and rhythm, will find the twists and turns in the younger writer's prose a refreshing surprise.

—PETER CONSTANTINE

A Vision (*Vision*)

"Prose Sketch"

1893

First printed in Der Frühlingsturm (Spring Storm), *Monthly for Art and Literature, edited by Paul Thomas [Mann], June/ July issue, 1893. First book publication in* Erzählungen [Stories], *Frankfurt, 1958. How can detached, analytical observation represent accurately but as literature the realm of distorted perception and the powerful, irrational sensations of a hallucination? This experiment grows out of the post-Nietzschean, early psychological interest of the time in applying a rigorous experimental method to representing states of feeling rather than merely quantifiable facts. This scientific interest in the irrational was a theme that remained with Mann throughout his career. It has prominent echoes in* The Magic Mountain, Doctor Faustus, *and* Felix Krull.

As I MECHANICALLY ROLL another cigarette and the speckles of brown dust tumble onto the yellow-white blotting paper of my writing folder, I find it hard to believe that I am still awake. And as the warm damp evening air, flowing in through the open window beside me, shapes the clouds of smoke so strangely, wafting them out of the light of the green-shaded lamp into matte black darkness, I am convinced I am dreaming.

How wild it is! My notion is snapping its reins on fantasy's back. Behind me the chair-back creaks, secretly nattering, sending a sudden shudder through all my nerve ends. It annoys me and disturbs my deep study of the bizarre shapes of smoke drifting around me, through which I had already resolved to draw a connecting thread.

Now the silence has gone to the dogs. Jangling movement flows through all my senses. Feverish, nervous, crazed. Every sound a stab! And tangled up in all this, forgotten things rise up. Things long ago imprinted on my sense of sight now strangely renew themselves, along with their old forgotten feelings.

With interest I notice that my awareness expands hungrily, embracing that area in the darkness in which the bright forms of smoke stand out with increasing clarity. I notice how my glance engulfs these things, only imaginings, yet full of bliss. And my sight takes in more and more, it lets itself go more and more, creates more and more, conjures more and more, more…and…more.

Now the creation, the artwork of chance, emerges, clear, just like in the past, looming from things forgotten, re-created, formed, painted by fantasy, that magically talented artist.

Not large: small. And not really a whole, but perfect, as it had been back then. And yet infinitely blurring into darkness in all directions. A world. A universe. In it light trembles, and a powerful mood, but no sound. Nothing of the laughing noises around it can penetrate: the laughing noises not of now, but of then.

Right at the base, dazzling damask. Across it, woven flowers zigzag and curve and wind. Translucently pressed upon it and rising up slender a crystalline goblet, half-filled with pallid gold. Before it, dreaming, a hand stretches out, the fingers draped loosely around the goblet's base. Clinging to one finger is a matte silver ring upon which a ruby bleeds.

Where the vision strives to form an arm above the delicate wrist, in a crescendo of shapes, it blurs into the whole. A sweet enigma. The girl's hand lies dreamy and still. Only where a light-blue vein snakes its way over its pearly whiteness does life pulse and passion pound, slowly and violently. And as it feels my glance it becomes swifter and swifter, wilder and wilder, till it turns into a pleading flutter: stop, don't…

But my glance is heavy and cruelly sensual, as it was then. It weighs upon the quaking hand in which, in the fight with love, love's victory pulsates…like then…like then.

Slowly, from the bottom of the goblet, a pearl detaches itself and floats upward. As it moves into the ruby's orbit of light it flames up blood red, and then on the surface is suddenly quenched. The disturbance threatens to dissipate everything, and my eyes struggle to rekindle the vision's soft contours.

Now it is gone, faded into darkness. I breathe, breathe deeply, for I notice that I had forgotten now, as I had back then…

I lean back, fatigued, and pain flares up. But I know now as surely as I did then: You *did* love me…Which is why I can cry now.

Fallen (*Gefallen*)

1894

First printed in Die Gesellschaft [Society], *October 10, 1894.*
First book publication: Erzählungen, *Frankfurt, 1958. This story is a biting assault on the nineteenth-century cliché of a sensitive, well-bred young man falling in love with an actress. The young man's intense feelings are seen from the detachment of distance and disillusion; the narration and the prominence of sensory imagery mark the introduction of psychology into romantic fiction.*

THE FOUR OF US had gotten together again.

This time little Meysenberg was the host. The dinners in his atelier were quite charming.

It was a strange space, decorated in a single style: the bizarre whimsicality of an artist. Etruscan and Japanese vases, Spanish fans and daggers, Chinese parasols and Italian mandolins, African shell-horns and antique statuettes, colorful rococo bric-à-brac and waxy Madonnas, old copper etchings and works from Meysenberg's own brush were all strewn about the room on tables, étageres, consoles, and over the walls, which, moreover, like the floors, were covered in thick oriental carpets and faded embroidered silks: everything thrown together in clashing confusions, which, so to speak, pointed their fingers at themelves. We were four: brown-haired, little, nimble Meysenberg; Laube, the very young, blond, idealistic economist who loudly championed women's liberation wherever he happened to be; Dr. Selten, and myself. The four of us were sitting together in the middle of the atelier on the most disparate kinds of seats around a heavy mahogany table. We had been addressing the superb repast that our ingenious host had put together, and more so the wine. Meysenberg had outdone himself again.

The doctor sat in a large, antique, carved church seat, constantly making fun of it in his sharp way. He was the ironic one among us: His disdainful bearing was full of both worldliness and contempt for the world. He was the oldest; he must have been around thirty. And he had "lived" more than we had. "He's wild!" Meysenberg said. "But he's amusing."

To some extent one could see that "wildness" in the doctor. His eyes had a certain blurry gleam, and his short, black hair was already thinning slightly on top. His face ended in a pointed, well-groomed goatee, and derisive, mocking expressions flitted from his nose down to the corners of his mouth, giving him at times a bitter mien.

By the time we reached the Roquefort we were already in the midst of one of our "deep discussions." Dr. Selten had coined this phrase with the dismissive scorn of a man who, as he himself said, had long since made it his one and only credo to enjoy this life, which the powers above seem to direct so haphazardly, unreservedly and to the fullest. He would shrug his shoulders and say: "Is there a better way?"

But Laube had in the meantime deftly steered the conversation onto his own territory and was again beside himself, gesticulating wildly in the air from his deep armchair.

"That's what I'm saying! That's exactly what I'm saying! It is the ignominious social status of the female," (he never said "woman," always "female," because it sounded more scientific) "rooted in the prejudices, the stupid prejudices of society!"

"Cheers!" Selten said very softly and compassionately, and emptied a glass of red wine. This pushed the young man over the brink. He jumped up.

"I can't believe it! I just can't believe it! You old cynic! It's impossible to talk to you! But you two," he challenged Meysenberg and me, "surely you must agree with me! Yes or no?"

Meysenberg peeled himself an orange.

"I would say fifty-fifty, most definitely!" he said confidently.

"Go on," I egged young Laube on. He had to let off steam, otherwise we would never hear the end of it.

"It's the stupid prejudices and bigoted injustice of society, is what I say! All those minor details—God, it's ridiculous. I mean, opening schools for girls and training females to be telegraph operators and such—what's that supposed to accomplish? But on the whole, in the big picture! What ideas! And from an erotic, sexual standpoint, what petty-minded cruelty!"

"Well," said the doctor, relieved, putting his napkin down. "At least things are perking up."

Laube didn't deign to look at him.

"Look," he continued vehemently, waving about a large after-dinner candy, which he then popped into his mouth with a grandiose gesture, "Look. If two people are in love and the man seduces the girl, then he remains as much a gentleman as before, and is even considered quite dashing—the dog! But the female is the doomed one, spurned by society, ostracized, fallen. Yes, *fal-len*! What is the moral reasoning behind such a notion? Isn't the man just as 'fallen'? Wasn't he more *dishonorable* than the female? ...Well, what do you think? Say something!"

Meysenberg looked pensively at the smoke of his cigarette.

"You do have a point," he said benevolently.

Laube's face lit up in triumph.

"Do I? Do I?" he kept repeating. "Where is the moral justification for such a judgment?"

I looked at Dr. Selten. He did not say a word. He was rolling a little ball of bread crumbs with his fingers, staring silently down at the floor with that bitter expression on his face.

"Let us rise," he said quietly. "I would like to tell you a story."

We moved the dinner table out of the way and settled down in the back of the room, in a cozy corner furnished with carpets and small sofas. A lamp hanging from the ceiling filled the room with a bluish twilight. A softly pulsing layer of cigarette smoke already hung in the air.

"Well, go on," Meysenberg said, filling four small glasses with his French Benedictine.

"Well, as the subject has come up, I'll gladly tell you this story," the doctor said. "Neatly packaged in full-blown story form. You know I used to dabble in such things."

I could not quite see his face. He sat leaning back in his chair, one leg over the other, his hands in the pockets of his jacket, and looked calmly up at the blue lamp.

34

*

The hero of my story, he began after a while, had graduated from the *Gymnasium* in his small north-German home town. When he was nineteen or twenty he attended the University of P., a town of considerable size in southern Germany.

He was the perfect "good fellow." It was impossible to be angry with him. Fun-loving and good-natured, he immediately became the favorite among his classmates. He was a slim, handsome young man, with soft facial contours, lively brown eyes, and gently curved lips, over which the delicate down of a mustache had already appeared. When he strolled through the streets, with his round straw hat perched on the back of his dark locks and his hands in his pockets, looking about briskly, the girls would glance at him adoringly.

And yet he was pure—in body and soul. He could say with General Tilly that he had never lost a battle and never touched a woman. In the first case, because he had not had the opportunity, and in the second case again because he had not had the opportunity.

Of course, he had been in P. for only two weeks when he fell in love. Not with a waitress, as is customary, but with a young actress, a Fräulein Weltner, a naive belle from the Goethe Theater.

With the intoxication of youth in him, as the poet wisely noted, a man will see Helen of Troy in every woman. But this girl really was beautiful: a childishly

35

delicate body, pale blond hair, gentle, merry gray-blue eyes, a dainty little nose, an innocently sweet mouth, and a round, soft chin.

First he fell in love with her face, then with her hands, then with her arms, which he saw bared in a classical role, and one day he loved her through and through. He even loved her soul, which he did not yet know at all.

His love cost him a fortune. At least every other night he took an orchestra seat at the Goethe Theater. He constantly had to write his mama for money, inventing the most reckless explanations. But he lied for his love's sake; that excused everything.

When he knew he loved her, the first thing he did was to write poetry. The well-known German "silent lyric." He often sat among his books late into the night, composing these poems. The small alarm clock on his dresser ticked monotonously, while outdoors from time to time lonely footsteps echoed. High up in his chest, where his neck began, he felt a soft, tepid, flowing pain that often tried to well up into his eyes. But as he was too ashamed really to cry, he merely cried in words onto the patient sheets of paper.

In plangent verse he expressed, with melancholy sounds, how sweet and lovable she was, and how tired and ill he was, and how his soul was in great turmoil, drifting far, far away towards a distant haze where sweet happiness slumbered among countless roses and violets; but he was bound, he could not reach it.

This was clearly ridiculous. Everybody would laugh. The words he wrote were so foolish, so insignificant and helpless. But he loved her! He loved her!

Of course, immediately after acknowledging his love he was ashamed of himself. It was such a pitiful, submissive devotion, in which he only wanted to quietly kiss her little foot, because she was so fine and lovely, or her white hand, and then gladly die. Of her mouth he did not even dare think.

Once, waking up in the middle of the night, he imagined her lying in her bed, her dear head resting on white pillows, her sweet mouth slightly open, and her hands, those indescribable hands with their dainty blue veins, crossed on the sheets. He suddenly turned over, pressed his face into his pillow, and wept for a long time in the darkness.

He had reached the breaking point. He could no longer write poetry and no longer eat. He avoided his friends, hardly went out, and had big dark rings under his eyes. He wasn't working at all any more, and couldn't bring himself to read. All he wanted to do was sit in front of her picture, which he had bought long ago, and languish wearily in tears and love.

One evening he was having a quiet glass of beer with his friend Rölling in the corner of a pub. They had been school friends, and Rölling was studying medicine too, but was several semesters ahead.

Suddenly Rölling set his beer mug down firmly on the table.

"All right! Tell me, what's the matter?"

"With me?"

He finally broke down and let it all out, about her, about himself.

Rölling shook his head critically.

"That's pretty bad! Well, there's not much you can do. You aren't the first. Totally unapproachable. Until recently she lived with her mother. The mother has been dead for a while, but still, there's nothing you can do. A disgustingly respectable girl."

"Why, did you think I would…"

"Well, I'd have thought, you at least hoped to…"

"Rölling!"

"Well…Oh. I'm sorry! Now I see what's going on. I wasn't thinking from the sentimental side. So send her a bouquet of flowers along with a demure and reverent note begging for permission to present yourself so you can express your admiration for her in person."

He turned quite pale and began trembling all over.

"But…but, I can't do that!"

"Why not? Any messenger will go for forty pfennigs."

He began trembling even more.

"Oh Lord, if that were possible!"

"Where does she live?"

"I…I don't know."

"You *don't know*? Waiter, the directory, please." Rölling quickly found her address.

"So then, all this time you've seen her living up in the clouds, now it's suddenly Heustrasse 6A, fourth floor;

see, here it is: Irma Weltner, member of the Goethe Theater…By the way, that's a pretty rundown neighborhood. That's what you get for being virtuous."

"Rölling, please!"

"All right, I'm sorry. So that's what you'll do, right? You might even get to kiss her hand, you poet! Tonight, put the money for the orchestra seat into a bouquet."

"Oh God, what do I care about the stupid money!"

"How fine it is to have taken leave of one's senses!" Rölling declaimed.

The very next morning a touchingly naive letter accompanied a breathtaking bouquet to the Heustrasse. If only he would receive an answer from her, any answer, he would shout with joy and kiss the words on the paper!

A week later the flap of the letterbox on his front door had broken off because of the constant opening and shutting. His landlady was furious.

The rings under his eyes had become deeper; he really looked miserable. When he looked in the mirror he was really shocked, and wept with self-pity.

"This can't go on!" Rölling finally said to him one day with great determination. "You're really going the way of the Decadents. You have to do something! Tomorrow just go and see her."

He stared at Rölling with big red eyes.

"You mean, just go…?"

"Yes."

"I can't do that! She hasn't given me permission!"

"That idea with the scribbling was stupid, anyway. We should have realized right away that she wouldn't answer a letter from someone she didn't know. You simply have to go yourself. You'll be floating on air even if she just says good morning to you. And it's not like you're some monster; she's not going to throw you out. Tomorrow you've got to go!"

He felt dizzy.

"I don't think can," he said quietly.

"Then you're a lost cause!" Rölling answered angrily. "You'll have to see how you're going to get over this on your own!"

Days of great inner strife followed as, outdoors, winter fought one last battle with the month of May. But one morning, after waking from a deep sleep in which he had seen her in his dreams, he opened his window and it was spring.

The sky was bright—bright blue—as if smiling gently, and the air was so sweetly spiced.

He felt, smelled, tasted, saw, and heard spring. All his senses were spring, and he felt as if the broad sunbeam which shone over the house was streaming into his heart with tremulous vibrations, bringing clarity and strength.

He silently kissed her picture, put on a clean shirt and his good suit, shaved off the stubble on his chin, and walked over to Heustrasse.

A strange, almost frightening peace had come over him. A dreamlike peace, as if it were not he himself climbing those stairs, stopping in front of the door, and reading the nameplate, Irma Weltner.

Suddenly he was overcome by the feeling that this was madness—what did he want?—and he thought of quickly turning around before anyone saw him. But it was as if with this final groan of his shyness he had at last shaken off his previous feverish state, and it had been replaced in his feeling by a powerful and spirited self-confidence. Up to this point he had felt weighed down by an oppressive necessity, as in hypnosis, but now he felt free, driven by an unerring, exulting will.

It was spring, after all!

The doorbell rang tinnily through the house. A maid came and opened the door.

"Is Mademoiselle at home?" he asked briskly.

"At home…yes…but who, may I ask…"

"Here you are."

He handed her his card, and as she walked off with it he simply followed right behind her, his heart brimming over with boisterous joy. When the girl handed the card to her young mistress he had already entered the room, and stood there confidently with his hat in his hand.

It was a room of average size with simple dark furnishings.

The young lady had stood up from her seat by the window. She seemed to have just put down the book that lay on a small table beside her. He had never seen her as charming on the stage as she now appeared to him in reality. Her gray dress with its darker breast-insert, clothed her fine figure with subdued elegance. The May sun trembled in the blond locks on her forehead.

His blood rushed and swirled with delight, and when

she looked at his card, astonished, and then at him with even more astonishment, he took two quick steps towards her as the deep yearning within him broke out into a few fearful, intense words:

"But no! You mustn't be angry with me!"

"This is quite an assault!" she said, amused.

"But I had to, even if you didn't give me permission, I had to tell you in person *how much* I admire you!"

With a smile she offered him a chair, and as they sat down he continued falteringly:

"You see, this is how I am, I'm the kind of person who needs to say what he feels, and not just...just keep everything bottled up inside, and this is why I asked.... But why didn't you answer my letter?" he interrupted himself naively.

"Oh," she answered smiling, "I can't tell you how genuinely happy I was when I got your kind letter and the beautiful bouquet. But...it would not have been proper for me to simply...how was I to know..."

"No, no, of course, I see what you mean, but I hope that you aren't angry that I went ahead without permission...?"

"How could I be angry?"

"You haven't been in P. long?" she added quickly, tactfully avoiding an embarrassing silence.

"A good six or seven weeks already."

"Such a long time? I thought that you only saw me on stage just over a week ago, when you sent your nice letter."

"Oh, Fräulein Weltner! Since I've been here I've seen you almost every evening! In every role you've played!"

"Then why didn't you come earlier?" she asked in innocent astonishment.

"Should I have come earlier?" he answered flirtatiously. He felt so indescribably happy sitting in the armchair opposite her, chatting warmly with her. The whole situation seemed so incredible to him that he almost feared that once again a sad awakening would follow this happy dream. He was so cheerful and at ease that he felt he could relax and comfortably cross his legs, and at the same time he was so transported with bliss that he could have thrown himself at her feet with a cry of joy…this is all such silly foolery! I love you…I love you!

She blushed slightly, but laughed heartily at his witty response.

"I'm sorry, you misunderstand me. I expressed myself rather awkwardly," she said. "But you mustn't take me so literally…"

"I shall try, from now on, to be less literal…"

He was ecstatic. That is what he told himself yet again after these words. She was sitting there in front of him! And he was sitting close to her! He kept pinching himself over and over, to convince himself that he was really there; his eyes, filled with bliss and disbelief, constantly darted over her face and figure…This was truly her pale blond hair, her sweet mouth, her soft chin with its gentle tendency to doubleness. This really was her bright, girlish voice, her delightful speech, which now, off-stage, allowed a hint of South German dialect to come through. Those were her hands, her beloved hands, which took his card once again from the table so she could scrutinize his name. Those hands, which in his dreams he had kissed so often, those indescribable hands! And her eyes, which were now looking at him again with a friendly interest that grew and grew. And it was to him that she was speaking as she continued the conversation, which at times came to a halt and at times flowed freely, on topics such as where they came from, their everyday lives, and Irma Weltner's stage roles. Of course he praised her interpretations to the skies, even though, as she herself laughingly admitted, there was precious little to "interpret" in her roles.

When she laughed there was always a small theatrical note in her voice, as if a rambunctious uncle had just told a bad joke; but it enthralled him as he watched her face with naive and frank ardor, which was so powerful that he more than once had to beat down the temptation to throw himself at her feet and candidly avow his deep, deep love for her.

A whole hour might have gone by before he looked at his watch in dismay and hastily got up.

"But I have taken up much too much of your time, Fräulein Weltner! You should have sent me away ages ago! You should be aware that in your presence, time…"

Without knowing it, he was being quite clever. He had shifted his loud admiration almost completely from

44

the young woman as artist; instinctively his naively pro-claimed compliments became more and more personal.

"But what time is it? How come you are leaving al-ready?" she asked in melancholy astonishment, which, if it was put on, was acted with more realism and per-suasiveness than anything she had ever done on stage.

"Dear God, I have bored you long enough! A whole hour!"

"Not at all! The time just flew by!" she cried with what was this time doubtlessly genuine astonishment. "A whole hour? I'm going to have to hurry, and drum in some of my new lines for tonight—will you be at the theater tonight? I was hopeless at the rehearsal. The director would have liked to beat me."

"When can I murder him?" he asked solemnly.

"The sooner the better!" she laughed, reaching out her hand to him in farewell.

He bent over her hand with surging passion, and pressed his lips against it in a long, insatiable kiss from which, even though deep inside he urged himself to cir-cumspection, he could not break away from the sweet perfume of her hand, from the blissful rush of emotion.

She withdrew her hand with some haste, and when he looked at her again he thought he noticed on her face a confused expression that perhaps should have made him ecstatic, but which he interpreted as anger at his unseemly behavior. For a moment he was deeply ashamed.

"My deepest thanks, Fräulein Weltner," he said

quickly and with more ceremony than previously, "for the great kindness that you have shown me."

"Not at all. I am very pleased to have met you."

"And may I ask a favor?" he said, again in his earlier candid tone. "You wouldn't refuse me…permission…to visit you again?"

"Of course!…I mean…certainly, why not?" She was somewhat embarrassed. After the strange way he had kissed her hand, the request seemed a little out of place.

"It would be a great pleasure to chat with you again," she added with calm friendliness, once more stretching out her hand to him.

"I am very grateful!"

He bowed quickly, and found himself outside. Now that she was no longer in front of him, he once more felt that it was a dream. But then he again felt the warmth of her hand in his and on his lips and knew that it had really happened, and that his rash, blissful dreams had become reality. He staggered down the stairs as if in a drunken stupor, leaning sideways over the balustrade which she must have touched so often, kissing it with ecstatic kisses—all the way down.

In front of the house, which was set slightly back from the street, there was a small garden-like yard, on the left side of which a lilac bush was opening its first blossoms. He stopped before it and plunged his hot face into its cool shrubbery, and for a long time, his heart pounding, drank in the fresh, delicate fragrance.

Oh,—oh, how he loved her!

When he entered the restaurant, Rölling and some other young friends had already finished their meal. Flushed, with a hasty greeting, he sat down beside them. He sat quietly for a few minutes, looking at them one by one with an overbearing smile, as if he were secretly making fun of them for sitting there in complete ignorance, innocently smoking their cigarettes.

"Hey!" he suddenly shouted, leaning forward over the table. "I have news for you! I'm happy!"

"Oh?" Rölling said, looking him meaningfully in the eye as he ceremoniously reached his hand to him over the table. "My most sincere congratulations!"

"What for?"

"What's going on?"

"Of course! You fellows don't know about it yet! It's his birthday today. He's celebrating his birthday! Look at him—doesn't he look reborn?"

"Really?"

"My word!"

"Congratulations!"

"Hey, you know you should…"

"Absolutely! *Waiter*!"

One had to admit that he knew how to celebrate his birthday.

After an interminable week, during which he waited with intense, yearning impatience, he called on her once more. She had, after all, given him permission. All the exalted *états d'âme* that had stirred his feelings during their first meeting had already vanished.

He began seeing her pretty often. Each time she kept allowing him to come again.

Their conversation flowed freely, and their meetings could almost be called warm and friendly, if a certain embarrassment and diffidence had not on occasion suddenly come between them; something like a vague anxiety, which usually affected both of them at the same time. At such moments the conversation would suddenly falter and lose itself in a fixed, silent gaze, which, like the first time he kissed her hand, made them continue for a time on a more correct and formal level.

Sometimes after a performance she allowed him to walk her home. What a fullness of unbridled happiness these spring evenings held for him, walking through the streets by her side! When they reached her door she would thank him cordially for his trouble, he would kiss her hand, and then take his leave with rejoicing thankfulness in his heart.

On one of these evenings, when after having said good-by and walked away a few paces he looked back, he saw that she was still standing by her front door. She seemed to be searching for something on the ground. And yet he had the impression that she had suddenly assumed that pose only after he had quickly turned around.

"I saw the two of you last night!" Rölling said one day. "My respects! Well done! No one has ever managed to get this far with her. Good job! But I must say you're also bit of a jackass. She can't make any more

overt advances to you than she's already making! What
a paragon of virtue you are! She must be head over heels
in love with you! You should just go for it!"

He looked at Rölling blankly for a second. Then he
understood, and shouted: "Oh shut up!"

But he was shivering.

*

Spring was drawing to a close. The end of this May
brought a row of hot days on which not a drop of rain
fell. The sky stared down at the thirsting earth with a
wan and misty blue, and the day's relentless, cruel heat
gave way by evening to a dull and oppressive sultriness,
made only heavier by a weak breeze.

On one of these late afternoons our young hero was
wandering alone in the hilly park outside the town. He
could not bear being at home. He felt ill again, impelled
anew by that yearning thirst which he thought had been
stilled by all his recent happiness. But now he was sighing again—sighing for her. What more did he want?

The answer came from Rölling, that more benevolent and less witty Mephistopheles:

> "So that the divine Inspiration—
> I may not say how—be consummated…"

He shook his head with a groan and stared into the
distant twilight.

The answer had come from Rölling! Or rather Rölling, seeing him once more pale and unhappy, had defined the situation that had been lost in the mists of his soft and hazy melancholy, and with brutal words had laid it out starkly before him.

He wandered on in the sultry heat, with a tired yet eager pace.

He could not find the jasmine whose perfume he had been inhaling all the while. But jasmine could not yet be in bloom! Yet since he had come outdoors, wherever he went, he smelled its sweet, numbing fragrance.

There was a curve in the path, and a bench leaning against a steep rockface on which there was a scattering of trees. He sat down and gazed straight ahead.

On the other side of the path the parched grassy embankment descended abruptly to the river, which flowed past sluggishly. Across the river, the highway ran in a straight line between two rows of poplars. Far away, on the washed-out lilac horizon, a solitary farmer's wagon was slowly moving.

He sat and stared, and as nothing around him was stirring he did not dare to move either.

And the sultry scent of jasmine hung ever-present in the air.

And the whole world lay under this heavy dullness, a lukewarm, oppressive silence so full of craving and thirst. He felt that some sort of release must be imminent, that a liberation was bound to come from somewhere, a tempestuously quenching relief of all this tremendous thirst in him and in nature.

And once more he saw the girl before him in a light classical costume, and saw her slender white arm, which surely must be soft and cool.

He stood up with a vague, half-hearted resolution, and walked faster and faster back towards town.

When he stopped, dimly aware that he had reached his goal, a terrible fear suddenly overcame him.

Evening had fallen. Everything around him was silent and dark. At this time, in this still thinly-settled area, hardly anyone was outdoors. The moon, almost full, stood in the sky among many softly veiled stars. Far away the phlegmatic light of a street-lamp glimmered.

He was standing in front of her house.

No, he hadn't intended to go there! But his yearnings had driven him there, without his realizing it.

Now that he was standing there, staring motionlessly up at the moon, he felt that this was good, that he was in the right place.

From somewhere there came more light, from upstairs, from the fourth floor, from her room, where a window stood open. So she wasn't performing at the theater. She was home and had not yet gone to bed.

*

He wept. He leaned against the fence and wept. It was all so sad. The world was so mute and parched, and the moon so pale.

He wept for a long time, for he felt for a while that this was the quenching release, the extinguishing, the liberation that he was seeking. But then his eyes were drier and hotter than before; the parched trepidation within him was crushing his whole body, making him gasp, gasp for…

Give in, give in.

No, don't give in! Pull yourself together! His body tightened. His muscles swelled. But then a soft, hushed pain washed away his strength again.

But why not, tired, just let go?

Weakly he pushed open the front door and with dragging feet slowly climbed the stairs.

Because of the hour the maid looked at him with astonishment, but she told him that Mademoiselle was home.

She did not even announce him—after a quick knock, he simply opened the door to Irma's living room.

He had no awareness of his actions. He did not walk up to the door, he just felt himself move. It seemed to him as if weakness had made him lose his grip, and as if he were now being guided solemnly, almost sadly by a silent necessity. He felt that any attempt at marshalling his will to direct this silent, powerful force would only generate harrowing strife within him. Give in—give in! What was right, what was necessary, would happen.

When he knocked he heard a slight cough, as if she were clearing her throat. Then she called out "come in" in a tired, questioning tone.

As he entered she was sitting on the sofa by the round table near the back wall of the dimly lit room. A shaded lamp stood on a small étagère by the open window. She did not look up, and as she seemed to think that it was only the maid she remained in her fatigued position, reclining with one cheek pressed against the cushion.

"Good evening, Fräulein Weltner," he said softly. She sat up with a start, and looked at him for a moment in great alarm.

She was pale, and her eyes were red. A gently pervasive expression of anguish lay on her lips, and an indescribably soft tiredness was in her pleading eyes as she looked up at him, and in her voice as she asked him: "So late?"

A feeling he had never had before welled up inside him, because he had never before forgot himself, so that he could see the warm, deep pain in her sweet, sweet face, and in those beloved eyes that had hovered over his life as a delightful, cheerful happiness. Before, he had really only felt pity for himself—but now he felt a deep, endlessly selfless pity for her.

He stood where he was, and asked her softly and shyly, his feelings echoing in the sounds: "Why were you crying, Fräulein Irma?"

She stared silently at her lap, at the white handkerchief she was holding tightly.

He went to her, and sitting down by her side took her slim, pale-white hands, which were cold and damp, and tenderly kissed each of them in turn. As hot tears surged up from his chest he repeated in a trembling voice: "You were…crying?"

She dropped her head even lower, so that the soft scent of her hair wafted towards him as her breast struggled with a heavy, frightened, inarticulate sorrow and her delicate fingers twitched in his. He saw two tears drop slowly and heavily from her long silky eyelashes.

Alarmed, he pressed her hands to his chest and cried out in desperate pain, his throat knotted: "I can't...I can't see you cry like this! I can't bear it!"

She lifted her delicate, pale face so they could look each other in the eyes and deep, deep into each other's souls, silently declaring in this glance their love for each other. Then a rejoicing, liberating, frantically exulting cry of love swept away the last shyness, and their young bodies embraced in violent writhing, their quaking lips pressing together, and into this first long kiss around which the world fell away, the fragrance of lilac, now sultry and insinuating, flooded through the open window.

He lifted her delicate, almost too-thin body from the sofa, and they stammered into each other's parted lips how much they loved each other.

But he felt a strange shudder at how she, who had been the goddess of his adoration, before whom he had always felt weak and awkward and small, now began to sway under his kisses.

*

He woke up once during the night.

The moonlight played in her hair, and her hand lay on his chest.

He raised his eyes to God and kissed her slumbering eyes and felt that he was a better fellow than he had ever been.

*

During the night there was a stormy downpour. Nature was released from its throbbing fever. The whole world breathed in a freshened fragrance.

Groups of mounted cavalry rode through the town in the cool morning sun, and people stood in front of their houses, breathing the good air and rejoicing. As he strolled happily back to his apartment through the rejuvenated spring, a blissful, dreamy slackness in his limbs, he felt like shouting "oh my sweet darling! Darling! Darling!" into the bright blue sky.

As he sat at his desk at home, contemplating her picture, he conscientiously set about examining his inner feelings, what he had done, and wondered whether, in spite of his complete happiness, he was no more than a scoundrel—which would have pained him greatly.

But everything was fine and beautiful.

He felt as tinglingly exhilarated as he had at his First Communion, and looking out into the chirping spring and the gently smiling sky he again felt, as he had during the night, as if he were looking into God's countenance with solemn and silent thankfulness. His hands came together, and with passionate tenderness he whispered her name into the spring in prayer.

Rölling—no, he could not tell him about it. Rölling was a good fellow, but he was sure to start talking the way he always did and make the whole thing look so—ridiculous. But when he went home again, one evening when the lamp was softly humming he would tell his dear mother all his bliss.

And he sank into it again.

*

Rölling, of course, knew within a week.

"Do you think I'm an idiot? I know all about it. You could at least fill me in on the details!"

"I have no idea what you're talking about. But even if I did, what would be the point of telling you something that you supposedly know about already?" he answered earnestly, looking at the questioner like a teacher and shaking his finger to underline the artful complexity of his sentence.

"Well, well, you're quite the joker! I hope you'll be happy!"

"I *am* happy, Rölling!" he answered seriously, warmly shaking Rölling's hand.

But things were again becoming too maudlin for Rölling.

"Tell me," he asked, "will Irma be playing the little

housewife? I'm sure she'll look charming in a bonnet! Can I play friend of the family?"

"Rölling, you're impossible!"

Perhaps Rölling was just talking through his hat. Perhaps too our hero's affair, which had completely estranged him from both his friends and his regular habits, could not in any case have remained secret for long. Word soon went around that "Fräulein Weltner from the Goethe Theater" was having an "affair" with a very young student, and people asserted that they had never really been convinced of "the young woman's" respectability.

Indeed, he was estranged from everything. The world around him had fallen away, and he floated through the air among fluffy pink clouds and little rococo cherubs with fiddles—bliss, bliss, bliss! If only he could lie at her feet forever, as the hours passed imperceptibly away and, with his head thrown back, drink in her breath from her mouth! For the rest, his life was over, over and done. All that was left was this one thing—the thing for which books only knew the paltry term "love."

The aforementioned position at her feet, by the way, was characteristic of the relationship between the two young lovers. It quickly demonstrated the external social superiority of a twenty-year-old woman over a man of the same age. He was always the one who, with the instinctive urge to please her, had to marshal his movements and words properly to respond to her. Aside from the complete abandon of their love scenes he was the one who, in their simple social relationship, could not be free and spontaneous. He let her chasten him like a child, partly out of tender love for her, but more because he was socially the lesser and weaker. Then, downcast and humble, he would beg her for forgiveness until she again allowed him to lay his head on her lap and ran her fingers through his hair with a motherly, almost pitying tenderness. Lying at her feet, he would look up to her; he came and went when she told him to; he catered to all her whims, and she did have whims.

"It looks like you're being henpecked," Rölling said. "I think you're too tame for this wild marriage."

"Rölling, you're an ass! You have no idea. You know nothing. I love her. It's as simple as that. I don't just simply love her...*that* way, but...I just love her, I...Oh, you can't express these things in words!"

"You're a fantastically fine fellow," Rölling said.

"What nonsense!"

What nonsense! These foolish expressions about being "henpecked" and "too tame" could only come from Rölling—he really had no idea what was going on. But what about himself? Where exactly did he stand? His relationship with her was so simple and perfect. He could always take her hands in his and constantly repeat: Oh, that you love me, that you love me just a little, I am so thankful to you for that!

*

Once on a beautiful soft evening, as he walked solitary through the streets, he again composed a poem that stirred him deeply. It went something like this:

When evening's light is on the wane
And daylight silently doth expire,
Then fold thy hands in gentle prayer
And raise thine eyes to our Heavenly Sire.

Doth not His benevolent, paternal eye
With sadness on our joy incline,
As if his silent gaze proclaims
That it will one day, alas, decline.

That oh, once spring hath run its course,
The baneful winter will come in,
That life's hard and bitter hand
Will fast chase bitter seasons in!

No! Lay not thy sweet fair brow
On mine so fearfully,
For green-leafed spring still laughs out loud,
As the sun's rays tremble brilliantly.

No! Cry not! For woe doth slumber far away.
O come unto my heart, come now!
For unto heaven in cheerful thanks
Love still can raise its brow.

It was not that this poem touched him because he truly and solemnly envisioned an inevitable end. That thought would have been total madness. It was only the very last lines that had come from deep within his heart, as the wistful monotony of their cadence was permeated by the quick free rhythms of his present happiness. The rest of the poem was really nothing more than a melodic mood which he allowed to bring a few vague tears to his eyes.

He again took to writing letters to his family at home, which surely no one understood. These letters didn't actually say anything, and yet they were vehemently punctuated, bristling with seemingly random exclamation marks. But somehow he had to express and disburse all his happiness, and deciding after some deliberation that he could not really be completely frank, he opted instead for the ambiguous exclamation marks. Often he felt like giggling to himself in silent bliss when he thought how even his learned father would not be able to make head or tail of these hieroglyphs that shouted out nothing more than: I am so very—very happy!

*

Until mid-July the days passed in this tender, foolish, sweet bubbling, happy way, and the story would have become boring if it hadn't been for a funny, amusing morning.

The day was truly ravishing. It was still quite early, about nine o'clock. The sun was still caressing. The air too smelled so fresh again—exactly as it had, he realized, on the morning after their first wondrous night together.

He was quite cheerful, and vigorously swung his walking stick on the clean white pavement. He was on his way to her.

The delicious thing was that she was not expecting him. He had planned to go to the university that morning, but then decided against it, for today. That was all he needed, to sit in a lecture hall in such splendid weather! If it had been raining, fine. But under these circumstances, under such a sky with its bright, laughing softness…to her! To her! This decision put him in a rosy mood. As he walked along the Heustrasse he whistled the boisterous rhythms of the drinking song from *Cavalleria Rusticana.* He stopped in front of her house for a while to drink in the fragrance of the lilacs. He had gradually developed a profound bond with this bush. Whenever he came by he would stop and engage it in a small, silent and extremely warm-hearted conversation. And the lilac would tell him in quiet, tender intimations of all the delights that awaited him. When, in the throes of intense happiness or sorrow, man despairs of confiding in another human being, he will often turn to nature to vent the overabundance of his emotions, which, in its mighty serenity, at times really seems to understand what's happening. He had long since come to see the lilac, with its inveterate, lyrical detachment, as an integral, sympathetic, and intimate part of his love—not simply a scenic prop in the novel he was living.

When he had allowed the beloved, soft fragrance sufficient time to finish its tale and its murmurs, he climbed the stairs. He left his walking-stick in the hall and in high spirits, without knocking, he cheerfully entered her living room, his hands in the pockets of his light summer suit and his round hat cocked back on his head, because he knew she liked him best when he wore it like that.

"Hello, Irma! I took you by..." "surprise," he was about to say, but he himself was surprised. As he entered the room he saw her rise from the table with a start, as if she hastily wanted to get something, but didn't quite know what. At a loss, she raised her napkin to her mouth, and stood there looking at him with remarkably wide-open eyes. There was coffee and cake on the table, on one side of which a dignified, elegantly dressed elderly gentleman with a white goatee was sitting chewing, staring at him dumbfounded.

Embarrassed, he quickly took off his hat and twisted it in his hands.

"Oh, excuse me, I didn't know you had company."

The elderly gentleman stopped chewing and turned to stare at the young woman.

Our hero was quite taken aback at how pale she had become, and how she was just standing there. But the elderly gentleman looked even worse—like a corpse! The little hair that he had left was disheveled. Who could this be? He racked his brains. A relative? But she had never said anything! Well, either way, he had come at a bad time. What a dreadful pity! He had so much been looking forward to this. Now he would have to leave again. It was horrible! And why wasn't anyone saying anything? How was he supposed to behave towards her?

"How come?" the elderly gentleman said suddenly, and looked about the room with his small, deep-set, shining gray eyes as if he were expecting an answer to this strange question. He must have been slightly off his head. The expression on his face was idiotic enough; his lower lip hung slack and feeble.

It suddenly occurred to our hero to introduce himself.

"My name is—. I merely…merely wanted to pay my respects…"

"What's that got to do with me?" the dignified elderly gentleman suddenly blustered. "What are you doing here?"

"Excuse me, but I…"

"Oh come on, you're in the way here! It's time you got going! Right, sweetie?" He gently smiled up at Irma.

Now our hero was not exactly a hero, but the elderly gentleman's tone was so totally offensive—not to mention that his disappointment had completely robbed him of his good mood—that he immediately changed his behavior.

"Begging your pardon, sir," he said quietly but firmly. "I do not see what gives you the right to take this tone with me, especially as I believe I have at least as much right to be in this room as you."

This was too much for the elderly gentleman. This was something he was not accustomed to. His lower lip wagged furiously with emotion, and he struck his napkin three times on his knee. Mustering the full power of his modest vocal faculties, he blurted out:

"You stupid young man! You stupid, stupid young man!"

If he who was so addressed had managed during the previous exchange to control his temper, and to keep in mind the possibility that the elderly gentleman might be some relation of Irma's, his patience was now at an end. The awareness of his position in the girl's life rose up proudly within him. He no longer cared who the other man was. He was deeply insulted, and insisting on what he considered his "domestic rights," he turned sharply towards the door and furiously demanded that the elderly gentleman leave the apartment.

The elderly gentleman remained speechless for a moment. Then he stammered between laughter and tears, his eyes straying around the room:

"Well…what…but…really! I say…! Lord,…what do *you* say to all of this?" He looked up imploringly at Irma, who had turned away without uttering a sound.

When the unfortunate old man, fully aware of the threatening impatience with which his opponent again pointed at the door, realized that no help was to be expected from Irma, he gave up.

"I shall leave," he said with noble resignation. "I shall leave immediately. But we will discuss this further, you rascal!"

"Definitely!" our hero shouted. "We most definitely will discuss this further! Or did you think, sir, that I was just going to take your insults! For the time being—get out!"

Quaking and groaning, the old man heaved himself up from his chair. His wide trousers hung loose about his bony legs. He grabbed his sides and almost fell back onto his chair. This made him maudlin.

"I'm just a poor old man!" he whimpered, as he hobbled to the door. "I'm such a poor, pitiful old man. What rascally rudeness! Oh—ah!" and a noble wrath again stirred within him. "But you wait! We will…We will discuss this! We will, we will!"

"We most definitely will!" his cruel tormentor assured him in the corridor, more amused than anything else, while the old gentleman put on his top hat with shaking hands, grabbed his heavy overcoat, and staggered to the stairs. "Yes we will…," the decent young man repeated quite softly; the old man's pitiful appearance began to fill him with compassion. "I am completely at your disposal," he continued politely, "but considering your behavior, you can hardly be surprised at mine." He bowed punctiliously and abandoned the elderly gentleman, whom he heard downstairs lamenting for a cab, to his fate.

It was only now that he again wondered who the crazy old man might be. Could he really be a relative? Her uncle or her grandfather? God, in that case he really had handled him too roughly. Perhaps the old gentleman was just naturally like that—so direct! But if that had been the case she could gave given him some sign! But she hadn't seemed to care. That struck him only now. Before, all his attention had been rivited on the insolent old man.—Who could he be? He felt quite uneasy, and hesitated for a moment before entering her room again, worried that he had perhaps behaved boorishly.

When he closed the door behind him, Irma was sitting sideways on the sofa, a corner of her batiste handkerchief between her teeth. She was staring rigidly straight ahead, and did not turn towards him.

For a moment he stood there completely bewildered. Then he clasped his hands together, and cried out, almost weeping with helplessness: "God, why don't you tell me who that was?"

Not a word. Not a movement.

Hot and cold shivers ran through him. He was overcome by a vague horror. But then he told himself that the whole thing was ridiculous, and sat down next to her, taking her hand protectively in his.

"Come, darling, be sensible. You're not mad at me, are you? It was the old man—he started it. Come on, who is he?"

Dead silence.

He stood up and distractedly walked a few steps away from her.

Near the sofa, the door which led to her bedroom was half open. All of a sudden he went in. Something on the table beside the unmade bed caught his eye. When he came back into the living room he held in his hand some blue notes, banknotes.

He was glad to have something else to talk about for the moment. He put the money on the table in front of her and said: "You should put this away. It was just lying there."

Suddenly he turned ashen. His eyes grew large, and his trembling lips parted. As he was returning with the banknotes in his hand she had looked up at him, and he had seen her eyes.

Something horrible inside him reached up with bony gray fingers and grabbed him inside of the throat. It was really sad to see how the poor young man stretched out his hands, and in the pitiful voice of a child whose toy is lying smashed on the floor, cried out over and over:

"Oh, no! Oh…oh, no!"

In pounding fear he rushed at her, blindly grabbing for her hands, as if to shelter her and to seek shelter with her, his voice desperately pleading:

"Oh no…! Please, please, no! You don't know— how…how I…no! Please, say no!"

Turning away from her he fell to his knees by the window, weeping loudly, and violently banged his head against the wall. The young woman stiffly pressed herself deeper into the corner of the sofa.

"Well, after all I do work in the theater. I don't know

why you're carrying on like this. Everyone does it. I'm tired of playing the saint; I've seen where that leads. It's no good. It's just no good in the theater. Virtue is fine for the rich; we have to look out for ourselves. There are clothes one has to…and, and all that." Finally she burst out: "But everyone knew I was…!"

He threw himself on her and covered her with horrifying, maniacal, scourging kisses. As he stammered: "Oh, you…you…!," it sounded as if all his love was struggling with frightful, clashing feelings.

Perhaps it was these kisses that taught him that from now on love was to be in hatred, and passion in wild revenge. Later, perhaps, one might turn into the other; he himself had no idea.

Then he found himself downstairs in front of the house by the lilac bush, under the soft, smiling sky. He stood there motionless for a long time, his arms hanging by his side. But suddenly he noticed once more the lilac's gentle loving breath surging towards him, tender, pure, and sweet.

And with a sudden movement of misery and rage he shook his fist at the smiling sky and violently plunged his hand into the treacherous fragrance, right to its core, snapping and breaking the bush and scattering its delicate blossoms.

Then he was sitting at home at his table, silent and weak.

Outside, a beautiful summer day shone with bright majesty.

He stared at her picture, where she still looked as sweet and pure as she had before.

Above thundering piano passages rolling through him a lone cello sang its strange lament. As the deep, soft tones, surging and swelling, enveloped his soul, some softly melancholy rhythms rose silently within him like an old, long-forgotten sorrow:

> That oh, once spring has run its course,
> The baneful winter will come in,
> That life's hard and bitter hand
> Will fast chase bitter seasons in!

The happiest ending I can give this story is that the poor fool could still cry.

*

For a moment there was complete silence in our corner. The two friends sitting beside me also seemed not unmoved by the melancholy mood the doctor's story had awakened in me.

"That's it?" little Meysenberg finally asked.

"Thank God!" Dr. Selten said with what seemed to me a somewhat feigned severity. He stood up and went over to a vase filled with fresh lilacs that stood on a small delicately-carved étagere in a faraway corner.

Suddenly I realized where the strangely potent impression that the tale had made on me had come: from these lilacs, whose fragrance had hung over the story and had played such an important role in it.

No doubt it had been this fragrance that had motivated the doctor to relate these events, and that had had such an insinuating effect on me.

"Touching," Meysenberg said, lighting a new cigarette with a deep sigh. "A most touching story. And so uncomplicated too!"

"Yes," I agreed. "And precisely this simplicity speaks for its truth."

The doctor gave a short laugh and leaned down closer to the lilacs.

The young blond idealist had not yet said a word. He kept the rocking chair in which he was sitting in constant motion, and went on eating after-dinner candies.

"Laube seems quite moved," Meysenberg noted.

"Well, the story *is* touching!" Laube answered eagerly. He stopped rocking and sat up straight. "But Dr. Selten was supposed to disprove my argument. As far as I can tell, he hasn't managed to. Even considering this story, what happens to the moral emancipation that a female…"

"Enough of your stale clichés!" the doctor interrupted brusquely, with an inexplicable agitation in his voice. "If you still haven't understood me I feel sorry for you. If a woman is swayed by love today, then tomorrow she's swayed by money. That's what I wanted to tell. Nothing more. That's perhaps where you'll find the moral emancipation you're so desperately clamoring for."

"But tell me," Meysenberg suddenly asked. "If this story is true, then how come you know it in such detail, and how come you're getting so worked up about it?"

The doctor was silent for a moment. Then he suddenly plunged his right hand with a short, jerky, almost convulsive movement into the lilacs, whose fragrance he had been breathing in deeply and slowly.

"For God's sake," he said, "because it was me—I was the 'good fellow.' Otherwise I wouldn't have given a damn!"

Truly—the way he said it, plunging his hand with sad and bitter brutality into the lilacs, just as he had in the story—truly, there was no trace left of the "good fellow."

The Will to Happiness

(*Der Wille zum Glück*)

1896

First printed in Simplicissimus, *August 22 and 29 and September 5, 1896. First book publication in* Der kleine Herr Friedemann: Novellen [Little Herr Friedemann, Novellas], *Berlin 1898. This is Thomas Mann's first artist story, a subject he treats from the point of view of literary modernism and social satire. This story contains the seeds of many important motifs that run through his fiction: the artist as the exotic product of mixed blood* (Tonio Kröger), *the artist as moralist of accomplishment* (Death in Venice), *the life of an artist as told by a school-friend* (Doctor Faustus). *The title is an odd echo of Nietzsche's notion of the life force, the "will to power." In Mann's view, the artist must die to life in order to live in art; the artist's "will to power" excludes the possibility of his personal happiness.*

OLD MR. HOFMANN had made his fortune as a plantation owner in South America. He had married a local woman of good family, and moved back to his native north Germany soon after. They lived in my home town, where the rest of his family resided. Paolo was born there.

I did not know his parents very well, but Paolo was the image of his mother. When I saw him for the first time, that is, when our fathers took us to school for the first time, he was a thin little fellow with a yellowish complexion. I can still see him now: In those days he wore his black hair in long locks, which, framing his narrow face, tumbled in disarray onto the collar of his sailor suit.

Since we had both been cosseted at home, we were somewhat less than pleased with our new surroundings, the bleak schoolroom, and in particular the shabby red-bearded individual who was intent on teaching us the ABC. Crying, I clung to my father's jacket as he was on the point of leaving, while Paolo remained totally passive. He leaned stiffly against the wall, pinching his narrow lips together, and with his large tear-filled eyes looked at the eager crowd of boys who were grinning boorishly and poking each other in the ribs.

Surrounded in this way by demons, we felt attracted to each other from the start, and were glad when the red-bearded schoolmaster let us sit next to each other. From then on we stayed together, mastered the basics of our education together, and traded sandwiches every day.

I recall that even then he was sickly. From time to time he was out of school for long periods, and when he returned the pale blue veins that one often sees in delicate, dark-haired people stood out even more clearly than usual on his temples and cheeks. This trait always stayed with him. It was the first thing I noticed when we met again here in Munich, and again later in Rome.

Our friendship lasted throughout our school years for somewhat the same reasons that it had begun. It was the "pathos of distance" that we felt towards most of our classmates, an emotion felt by all those who at fifteen secretly read Heine and pass judgment on the world and mankind.

We also took dancing lessons together—I think we were sixteen—and as a result we both fell in love for the first time.

He admired the little girl, a blond, cheerful creature who had smitten his heart, with a melancholy ardor that was remarkable for his age, and which sometimes seemed to me almost uncanny.

I remember one dance evening in particular. The girl granted another partner two cotillion dances in quick succession, but none to him. I watched him with apprehension. He was standing next to me, leaning against the wall, staring motionlessly at his patent leather shoes, when suddenly he fainted. He was taken home and lay ill in bed for a week. It turned out—I believe this was when they found out—that his heart was not of the healthiest.

Even before this he had begun drawing, and developed a considerable talent. I have kept a sheet of paper with a quick charcoal sketch of a face much like that girl's, signed "You are like a flower! Paolo Hofmann fecit."

I don't remember exactly when it happened, but we were in our last year in school when his family moved to Karlsruhe, where old Mr. Hofmann had connections. They did not want Paolo to change schools, and so put him up to board with an old tutor.

This arrangement, however, did not last long. Even if the following incident was not the direct cause for Paolo following his parents to Karlsruhe, it certainly had something to do with it.

During our religion class the tutor in question strode up to him with a withering stare, and from under the Old Testament that lay in front of Paolo pulled out a sheet of paper depicting a buxom female figure, fully sketched except for her left foot, exposing herself to view with no sense of shame.

So Paolo went to Karlsruhe and we occasionally exchanged postcards, a correspondence that little by little petered out.

About five years after we parted, I ran into him again

in Munich. I was walking down the Amalienstrasse one fine spring morning when I saw someone coming down the steps of the Academy, who from a distance looked almost like an Italian figurine. When I came nearer, it really was he.

He was of average height, slender, his hat tilted back on his thick black hair, his yellowish complexion threaded with little blue veins. He was elegantly but carelessly dressed—some buttons on his jacket, for instance, had been left unbuttoned—and his short mustache was lightly twirled. He came towards me with his swaying, indolent gait.

We recognized each other at about the same moment and greeted each other warmly. He seemed to be in an elated, almost exalted mood there in front of the Café Minerva as we questioned one another about the past five years. His eyes shone and he gesticulated a great deal. But he looked bad, really ill. It is easy for me to say that now with hindsight, but I really did notice it at the time, and even told him so.

"Oh, do I still look ill?" he asked. "I can believe it. I've been sick a lot. Last year, as a matter of fact, even critically ill. It's here."

With his left hand he pointed to his chest. "My heart. It's always been like this—but lately I've been feeling very well, extremely well. I'd say I'm completely healthy. I mean, it would be pretty sad if at twenty-three I wasn't!"

He was in high spirits. With cheerful animation he told me about his life since we had parted. He had convinced his parents to allow him to become an artist soon afterwards, had graduated from the Academy a little less than a year ago—it was by chance that he had just dropped in there. He had traveled for some time, lived in Paris for a while, and about three months ago had settled down here in Munich.

"Maybe for a long time—who knows? Maybe for ever..."

"Oh?" I asked.

"Well, why not? I like the city; I like it a lot. The whole tone, you know. The people, too! And what's also important, here a painter's social position is superb, even an unknown painter's. There's nowhere better..."

"Have you met any interesting people?"

"Yes; not many, but very pleasant. I must introduce you to one particular family; I met them during carnival. Carnival here, by the way, is charming! Their name is Stein. Baron Stein, no less."

"What kind of aristocracy is that?"

"What you might call cash nobility. The Baron was a stockbroker; he used to be a big shot in Vienna, mixed with all kinds of royalty, and so on. Then he suddenly fell on bad times, but managed to get out with—they say—about a million. Now he lives here, modestly but with style."

"Is he a Jew?"

"I don't think so. His wife, though, probably is. But I must say, they are extremely fine, pleasant people."

"Are there children?"

79

"No—that is to say—a nineteen-year-old daughter. The parents are very charming..."

He seemed embarrassed for a second, and then added: "I most definitely propose to introduce you to them. I would be delighted. Don't you agree?"

"Of course. I would be grateful to you; if only for making the acquaintance of this nineteen-year-old daughter—"

He looked at me from the side and said:

"Well, good. Let's not put it off too long. If you like, I'll drop by and pick you up tomorrow at about one o'clock, or one-thirty. They live at 25 Theresienstrasse, on the second floor. I look forward to bringing along an old school friend. It's arranged!"

The following day in the early afternoon we rang the bell of an elegant second-floor apartment in the Theresienstrasse. Next to the bell, it said "Baron von Stein" in bold, dark letters.

On the way, Paolo had been continually excited and almost deliriously high-spirited; but now, as we waited for the door to open, I noticed a peculiar change in him. Except for a nervous twitch of his eyelids, everything about him was totally still—violently, tensely still. His head was tilted slightly forward. The skin on his forehead was taut. He almost gave the impression of an animal desperately pricking up its ears, listening with all its muscles tensed.

The butler went off with our cards and returned, asking us to wait for a few moments; the baroness would appear momentarily. He opened the door to a medium-sized, darkly-furnished room.

As we entered, a young lady in a bright spring dress stood up in the bay-window from which one could gaze out into the street, and looked at us for a moment questioningly. "The nineteen-year-old daughter," I thought, glancing involuntarily at my companion out of the corner of my eye, and he whispered to me: "The young Baroness Ada!"

She was an elegant figure, mature for her age, and her soft, almost lethargic, movements were hardly in keeping with one so young. Her hair, which she wore over the temples with two curls falling over her forehead, was jet-black, and formed an effective contrast to the pale whiteness of her complexion. Her face, with its full, moist lips, fleshy nose, and black, almond-shaped eyes above which dark soft eyebrows curved, did not allow the slightest doubt that she was at least partially of Semitic extraction, but was of quite unusual beauty.

"Oh...visitors?" she asked, moving a few steps towards us. Her voice was slightly husky. She raised a hand to her forehead as if to see better, while with the other she leaned on the grand piano that stood against the wall.

"And very welcome visitors," she added in the same tone, as if she had only just now recognized my friend. Then she glanced inquisitively at me. Paolo approached her and, with the slow intensity with which one relishes an exquisite pleasure, he silently bowed his head over the hand that she reached out to him.

"Baroness," he said. "Will you permit me to introduce my old school friend, with whom I learned my ABC..."

She held out her hand to me, a soft, unadorned, seemingly boneless hand.

"A pleasure," she said, her dark, slightly tremulous eyes resting on me. "My parents will be delighted too...I hope that they have been told."

She sat down on the ottoman, while the two of us sat opposite her on chairs. As she talked, her white, flaccid hands rested in her lap. Her full sleeves barely reached below the elbows. I noticed the soft jointure of her wrists.

After a few minutes the door to the adjacent room opened and her parents entered. The Baron was an elegant, stocky, balding man with a gray goatee; he had an inimitable way of flicking the thick gold bracelet he was wearing back up into his cuff. It was not easily ascertainable whether, on the occasion of his advancement to the peerage, a few syllables of his name had fallen by the wayside; his wife, in contrast, was simply an ugly little Jewess in a tasteless gray dress. Large diamonds sparkled on her ears.

I was introduced and welcomed with great cordiality, while my companion was greeted like an old family friend.

After a few general questions about who I was and where I was from, the conversation moved on to an exhibition in which Paolo had a painting, a female nude.

"A really superb piece!" the Baron said. "The other

day I stood before it for half an hour. The flesh-color tone against the red carpet is extraordinarily effective. Yes, yes, our Mr. Hofmann!" And he patted Paolo patronizingly on the shoulder. "But don't work too hard, my dear boy, I beg you! It is of the utmost importance that you take care of yourself. How is your health?—"

While I was telling the Baron and his wife about myself, Paolo had been exchanging a few quiet words with young Baroness Ada, who sat close opposite him. The strangely intense calm that I had noticed in him before was still very much present. He gave, I can not say why, the impression of a panther ready to pounce. The dark eyes in his narrow yellowish face had such a sickly brightness in them that I was deeply moved when he answered the Baron's question in the most confident tone:

"Oh, so nice of you to ask! I'm in the best of health! I feel absolutely fine!"

When we stood up about a quarter of an hour later, the Baroness reminded Paolo that in two days it would be Thursday, and that he should not forget her five-o'clock tea. She also said that I should be so kind as to keep her Thursday teas in mind...

On the street Paolo lit a cigarette. "Well?" he asked. "What do you think?"

"Oh, they are extremely nice people," I answered quickly. "I was specially impressed by the nineteen-year-old daughter."

"Impressed?" He laughed abruptly and turned his head away.

"You laugh!" I said. "But while we were there I felt as if a secret yearning was troubling your glance. Am I wrong?"

He remained still for a moment. Then he slowly shook his head.

"I have no idea what could have led you..."

"Oh, really! My only question is, does Baroness Ada also feel..."

He looked silently down again for a moment. Then he said, quietly and confidently:

"I believe that I will be happy."

I took my leave from him, shaking him heartily by the hand, though I could not suppress a feeling of doubt.

Several weeks went by, during which I would occasionally go with Paolo for afternoon tea to the Baron's house. A small but quite pleasant circle gathered there: a young actress of the Imperial Theater, a doctor, an officer—I don't remember them all.

I did not notice any changes in Paolo's behavior. Although his appearance gave cause for concern, he was usually very happy and spirited, and whenever he was near the young Baroness he would again fall into the same strange calm that I had noticed the first time.

Then one day—I had not seen Paolo for two days— I met Baron von Stein in the Ludwigstrasse. He was on horseback, pulled up the reins, and held out his hand to me from the saddle.

"How nice to see you! I hope you will be dropping by tomorrow afternoon!"

"It would be a pleasure, Baron, even though I have a feeling that my friend, Mr. Hofmann, won't be coming by to pick me up..."

"Hofmann? But didn't you know—he has left! I thought he surely would have told you."

"No, not a word!"

"All quite *à bâton rompu*...the artistic temperament, you know...well, tomorrow afternoon!"

He set off on his horse and left me standing quite at a loss.

I rushed to Paolo's apartment.—Yes, I was told, unfortunately Mr. Hofmann has left. He did not leave an address.

It was obvious that the Baron knew that it was more than just "artistic temperament." And his daughter confirmed what I already had pretty much suspected.

This happened on an outing in the Isar valley which they had arranged and to which I had also been invited. It was already afternoon when we set out, and on our way back late in the evening Baroness Ada and I found ourselves walking together behind the others.

Since Paolo's disappearance I had not noticed any kind of change in her. She had remained completely calm and had not mentioned a single word about my friend, while her parents continuously expressed their regret at his sudden departure.

Now we were walking next to each other through one of the most charming areas around Munich. The moonlight shimmered through the foliage and we listened silently for a while to the voices of the rest of the party, which were as monotonous as the water foaming past us.

Suddenly, in a sure, steady tone, she began speaking of Paolo.

"You have been his friend since you were very young?" she asked.

"Yes, Baroness."

"You share his secrets?"

"I believe that I know his deepest secret, even though he has not told it to me himself."

"Then I can confide in you?"

"Of course, that goes without saying, Baroness."

"Very well then," she said, lifting her head with determination. "He asked for my hand in marriage and my parents turned him down. He is ill, they told me, very ill—but *I* don't care, I love him. I can confide in you, is that not so? I…"

She became flustered for a moment, but then continued with the same resolution.

"I do not know his whereabouts, but you have my permission the moment you meet him again to repeat the words he has already heard from my mouth, to write him those words the moment you find out his address: I will never accept another man's hand in marriage but his—Oh, we shall see!"

Along with defiance and determination, this last exclamation was so full of helpless pain that I couldn't help grasping her hand and silently pressing it.

So I turned to Hofmann's parents and in a letter asked them to let me know his whereabouts. I received an address in South Tirol, but the letter I sent there came back with a notice that the addressee had moved without leaving a forwarding address.

He did not want to be disturbed by anyone—he had run away from everything in order to die somewhere in complete solitude. Certainly, to die. After all, knowing what I did I had to accept the sad likelihood that I would never see him again.

Was it not clear that this hopelessly ill man loved this young girl with the same silent, volcanic, glowingly sensual passion that he had had in his earlier youth? The egoistic instinct of the sick person had kindled in him the desire to unite with radiant health; and wouldn't this fire, unquenched as it was, devour his last strength?

Five years went by without my receiving any sign of life from him, or any notification of his death, either.

Then last year I was in Italy, staying in and around Rome. I had spent the hot months in the mountains, and returned to the city at the end of September. One warm evening I was sitting over a cup of tea at the Café Aranjo, leafing through my newspaper and glancing absent-mindedly at the lively bustle of the large, brightly-lit space. Customers came and went, waiters rushed back and forth, and here and there the long-drawn-out calls of newsboys sounded through the wide-open doors.

Suddenly I see a man of about my age moving slowly between the tables towards an exit...That walk! Then he turns his head towards me, lifts his eyebrows, and comes over with an amazed and joyful "Ah!"

"You, here?" we both called out at the same time, and he added: "So we're both still alive!"

His eyes wandered a little as he said it. He had hardly changed in these five years, but his face seemed slightly gaunter, his eyes lay even deeper in their sockets. From time to time he inhaled deeply.

"Have you been in Rome long?" he asked.

"Not in the city. I was out in the country for a few months. And you?"

"I was at the seashore until a week ago. You know, I've always preferred it to the mountains...Yes, since we last met I've seen quite a bit of the world..."

And sitting next to me he started telling me over a sorbet how he had spent the last few years, traveling, always traveling. He had rambled in the mountains of Tirol, slowly crossed all of Italy, had gone to Africa from Sicily, and spoke of Algiers, Tunisia, Egypt.

"Finally, I spent some time in Germany," he said, "in Karlsruhe. My parents really wanted to see me, and were reluctant to let me leave again. Now I've been back in Italy for a few months. You know, I really feel at home here in the south. I like Rome above all!"

I hadn't mentioned a word about the state of his health. Now I asked him: "From what you say I take it that your health has become a good deal stronger?"

He looked at me for a moment, puzzled, and then answered:

"You mean, because I roam about so much? Oh, let me tell you, it's a natural instinct. What am I supposed to do—I've been forbidden to drink, smoke, love—I have to have some kind of drug. Do you understand?"

As I remained silent he added:

"Especially in the last five years!"

We had come to the subject that we had been avoiding, and the ensuing silence revealed that we were both at a loss. He leaned back on the velvet cushion and looked up at the chandelier. Then he said suddenly:

"You know, I really hope you'll forgive me for not getting in touch for so long…you understand, don't you?"

"Of course!"

"You are acquainted with what happened in Munich?" he continued in a tone of voice that was almost hard.

"Yes, totally. Actually, I've been carrying a message for you around with me all these years. A message from a lady."

His tired eyes flared up for a moment; then he said in the same dry, sharp tone as before:

"Let's hear if it's anything new."

"New? Hardly. Just a confirmation of what you already heard from her yourself…"

And in the midst of the noisy, gesticulating crowd I repeated the words that the young Baroness had spoken to me on that evening.

He listened, slowly running his fingers over his forehead. Then he said, without the slightest sign of emotion:

"Thank you."

The tone of his voice was beginning to confound me.

"But years have flowed over these words," I said. "Five long years, which she and you have both lived through…. Thousands of new impressions, feelings, thoughts, aspirations…"

I broke off, for he sat up and, in a voice once again trembling with a passion that for a moment I thought had been quenched, he said:

"I *stand by* those words!"

At that moment I recognized once more on his face and in his whole bearing the expression I had observed on the day when I was about to meet the young Baroness for the first time: that violent, frantically strained calm of a predator ready to pounce.

I changed the subject and we spoke again of his travels, of his few and occasional studies along the way. He seemed quite casual about it.

Shortly after midnight he rose.

"I want to go to sleep, or at least be alone…. You'll find me tomorrow morning at the Galleria Doria. I'm copying Saraceni; I have fallen in love with the musical angel. You'll come, won't you? I'm very glad that you're here. Good night."

And he left the café—slowly, quietly, with a heavy, dragging walk.

Throughout the following month I strolled through the city with him: Rome, the effusively rich museum of all the arts, the modern metropolis in the South, the city that is so full of loud, quick, hot, sensory life, but through which the warm wind carries over the sultry heaviness of the Orient.

Paolo's behavior always remained the same. Most of the time he was solemn and quiet; occasionally he would sink into a limp fatigue. Suddenly, with flashing eyes, he would pull himself together and energetically resume a fading conversation.

I must mention a day on which he let slip a couple of words whose significance has only now become fully clear to me.

It was on a Sunday. We had spent the glorious late summer morning walking along the Via Appia and now, after having followed the ancient thoroughfare far into the outskirts, we were resting on that small hill surrounded by cypress trees from which one can take in an enchanting view of the sunny Campagna, with the great aqueduct and the Alban hills wrapped in a soft haze.

Paolo was lying next to me on the warm grass, his chin in his hand, gazing into the distance with tired, misty eyes. Then there was again that movement in which he suddenly shook himself out of his total apathy, and turning to me said:

"It's the aura in the air—the aura!"

I murmured something in agreement, and we fell silent again. Then all at once, without warning, he turned his face to me and said ardently:

"Tell me, aren't you surprised that I'm still alive?"

Stunned, I did not say a word, and he again gazed with a thoughtful expression into the distance.

"I'm surprised myself," he continued slowly. "I wonder about it every day. Do you know what condition I'm in?—the French doctor in Algiers told me: 'Damned if I know why you still want to be traveling around! I advise you to go home and go to bed!' He could always say things like that because we played dominoes together every evening.

"I am still alive. Every day I'm almost at the end of my rope. At night I lie in the dark—on my right side, by the way! My heart pounds up into my throat, my head reels, and I break out in a cold sweat, and then I suddenly feel as if death were touching me. For a moment I feel as if everything inside me were standing still: my heart stops beating, my breath fails. I jump up, turn on the light, breathe deeply, look around, and devour everything with my eyes. Then I take a sip of water and lie down again—always on my right side! Slowly I fall asleep.

"I sleep deep and long, because I'm actually always dead tired. Would you believe that if I wanted to I could just lie down here and die?

"I think that in these last few years I have seen death a thousand times face to face. I did not die. Something holds me back. I jump up, I think of something, I hang onto a sentence that I repeat twenty times while my eyes hungrily drink in all the light and life around me…Do you understand what I'm saying?"

He lay quietly, as if he was not really expecting an answer. I no longer remember what I said to him, but I will never forget the impression his words made on me.

And then came the day—oh, I feel it as if it were yesterday!

It was one of the first days of autumn, one of those gray, sinister hot days on which a sultry and oppressive wind from Africa sweeps the streets. In the evening the whole sky trembles incessantly with sheet lightning.

That morning I had stopped by to pick Paolo up for a walk. His large suitcase stood in the middle of the room; the wardrobe and the bureau of drawers were wide open. His watercolors from the Orient and the plaster cast of the Vatican's head of Juno were still in their places.

He was standing rigidly by the window and continued looking out motionlessly when I called out to him in surprise. Then he turned to me abruptly, handed me a letter, and simply said:

"Read it."

I looked at him. On his narrow, yellowish, ill face with those black feverish eyes there lay an expression such as only death could bring, a tremendous solemnity, which made me lower my eyes to the letter that I had taken into my hand. I read:

"Dear Mr. Hofmann,

"Your parents were so kind as to inform me of your address, and I hope that you will receive this letter of mine in a generous spirit.

"Please allow me, dear Mr. Hofmann, to assure you that in the past five years I have entertained only the warmest sentiments of friendship towards you. If I were to think that your sudden departure on that day which was so painful for us both might have been induced by anger towards me and my family, it would make my sadness even stronger than the shock and surprise I felt when you asked me for my daughter's hand in marriage.

"I spoke to you frankly, from one man to another, expressing openly and honestly, at the risk of seeming blunt, the reasons why I was not able to offer my daughter's hand to a man who, I cannot emphasize enough, I have always thought so highly of in every respect. I spoke to you as a father who must consider his only child's lasting happiness, a father who would have stopped such budding desires the moment he seriously believed in their possibility.

"I address you today again, my dear Mr. Hofmann, in the same double capacity as a friend and father. Five years have gone by since your departure, and if in the past I had not had sufficient leisure to realize how deep was the affection that you instilled in my daughter, a recent event has completely opened my eyes. Why should I hide it from you? My daughter, thinking of you, declined the proposal of a fine gentleman, an excellent match that I, as her father, could only eagerly encourage.

"The years have passed, powerless to affect my daughter's feelings and wishes, and I ask you openly and with humility, should you, my dear Mr. Hofmann, still feel the same way about my daughter, then I hereby declare that we, her parents, no longer wish to stand in the way of our child's happiness.

"I look forward to your response with thankfulness, whatever it may be, and can only add my humblest respects.

Most Sincerely,
Baron Oskar von Stein

*

I looked up. He had put his hands behind his back and turned again to face the window. I simply asked him:

"Are you going?"

Without looking at me he answered:

"My things will be packed by tomorrow morning."

The day passed with errands and packing. I helped him, and in the evening I suggested we go for a last walk through the streets of the city.

It was still almost unbearably oppressive, and every second the sky flared up in a violent phosphorescent glow. Paolo seemed tired and calm—but he was breathing deeply and heavily.

We walked about for a good hour, either in silence or in trivial conversation, until we stopped in front of the Fontana di Trevi, the famous fountain with the galloping team of horses.

For a long time we gazed once again in wonder at the marvelous, spirited group that seemed almost magical, incessantly flooded with an incandescent blue. Paolo said:

"I am enchanted by Bernini, even in the work of his students. I don't understand his enemies. Even if his Last Judgment is more sculpted than painted, his work as a whole is more painted than sculpted. But can you tell me of anyone who is more brilliant with ornament?"

"By the way, do you know the story behind the fountain?" I asked. "Those who drink from it before leaving Rome will come back. Here is my traveling cup—" and I filled it from one of the jets of water. "You *shall* see your Rome again!"

He took the glass and lifted it to his lips.

At that moment the whole sky flared up in a blinding, drawn-out flash, and the glass smashed to pieces on the edge of the fountain.

With a handkerchief, Paolo patted the water from his suit.

"I'm feeling nervous and awkward," he said. "Let's go on. I hope the glass wasn't expensive."

By the next day the weather had cleared up. A light-filled blue summer sky stretched exuberantly over us as we drove to the station.

Our farewell was short. Paolo shook my hand silently as I wished him happiness, all the happiness in the world.

I stood on the platform for a long time, watching him stand rigidly by the wide train window. In his eyes I saw deep solemnity—and triumph.

What more can I say?—He is dead. He died the morning after the wedding night—almost during the wedding night.

This is the way it had to be. Was it not simply will, the will to happiness, that had enabled him to keep death at bay for such a long time? He had to die, die without a fight, without resistance, once his will to happiness was satisfied. He no longer had a pretext to live.

I asked myself whether he had acted badly, if he had been consciously irresponsible towards her whom he had bound to himself. But I saw her at the burial standing at the head of his coffin, and I recognized on her countenance the expression that I had found on his: the somber, strong solemnity of triumph.

Death (*Der Tod*)
1897

First printed in Simplicissimus, *January 16, 1897. First book publication:* Der kleine Herr Friedemann. *Showing traces of Nietzsche and Storm, this story contains motifs that will recur later in Mann's work: the death of a beloved child before the hero* (Doctor Faustus), *the association between the sea and death (e.g.* Death in Venice), *and Lisbon* (The Confessions of Felix Krull). *The oddity of this story results from its having been submitted for a* Simplicissimus *competition that called for a story "in which sexual love plays no role." Another writer, Jakob Wassermann, won first prize, but Mann's story was printed as well.*

September 10th.

Autumn has now arrived and summer will not re-
turn; I will never see summer again...

The sea is gray and silent, and a fine, mournful rain
is falling. Seeing this in the morning, I bade summer
farewell and greeted autumn, my fortieth autumn, which
has now relentlessly descended upon me. And relentlessly this autumn will bring with it the day whose date I
sometimes quietly whisper to myself with a feeling of
reverence and silent horror....

September 12th.

I went for a short walk with little Asuncion. She is a
good companion, silent, sometimes looking up at me
with large and loving eyes.

We went along the beach toward Kronshafen, but
we turned back in time before we had encountered more
than one or two people.

As we walked back, I looked at my house with pleasure. How well I had chosen it! Simple and gray, on a

cliff with damp and withered grass and a path that has become overgrown, it looks out over the gray sea. Behind the house runs the highway, and further back there are fields. But I pay no attention to them: I have eyes only for the sea.

September 15th.

Under the gray sky this lonely house on the cliff by the sea is like a gloomy, mysterious fairy-tale. And that is how I want it to be, in this, my last autumn. But this afternoon, as I was sitting by the window of my study, a car arrived with provisions. Old Franz helped with the unloading, and there was noise and the sound of voices. I can not express how much this disturbed me. I trembled with disapproval: I had ordered that these things only be done early in the morning, when I am asleep. Old Franz said: "As you wish, your Lordship." But he looked at me, his eyes inflamed, with anxious apprehension.

How could he understand me? He does not know.

I do not want ordinariness and boredom to touch my last days. I am fearful that death might have something bourgeois and mundane about it. I wish to feel alien and strange on that big, solemn, enigmatic day—the twelfth of October…

Death

September 18th.

In the last few days I have not gone out, but spent most of the time lying on the chaise longue.

I could not read very much either, because my nerves tormented me. I simply lay still and looked out into the slow, incessant rain.

Asuncion came to me often, and once she brought me flowers, a few withered, wet plants that she had found on the beach. When I kissed the child to thank her, she cried because I was "ill." How painfully her tender and melancholy love pierced my heart!

September 21st.

I sat for a long time by the window in my study, with Asuncion on my knee. We looked out at the wide gray sea, and behind us the large chamber with its high white doors and stiff-backed furniture lay in profound silence. And as I slowly caressed the child's hair that flowed straight and black down onto her tender shoulders, my thoughts went back to the whirling, colorful life I had led. I thought of my quiet and protected youth, of my travels through the whole world, and of the short, bright time when I was happy.

Do you remember the graceful and tenderly bright creature under the velvet sky of Lisbon? Twelve years have passed since she bore you this child and died as her slim arm lay around your neck.

She has her mother's dark eyes, litte Asuncion, only they are more tired and more pensive. But most of all she has her mouth, that infinitely soft and yet somehow sharply outlined mouth that is most beautiful when it is silent, smiling softly.

My little Asuncion! If you knew that I will have to leave you. Were you crying because I was "ill"? Oh, what does *that* have to do with it? What does *that* have to do with October the twelfth?...

September 23rd.

Days in which I can think back and lose myself in memories are few. For how many years have I only been able to think forward, waiting for this great and terrifying day, the twelfth of October of my fortieth year!

How will it be, how is it going to be? I am not afraid, but I see it approaching with agonizing slowness, this twelfth of October.

September 27th.

Old Doctor Gudehus came over from Kronshafen.

He came by car on the road and had lunch with Asuncion and me.

"It is most important," he said eating half a chicken, "that you exercise, your Lordship, exercise as much as possible in the fresh air. No reading! No thinking! No brooding! I have the impression that you are a philosopher, ho, ho!"

Well, I shrugged my shoulders and thanked him cordially for his trouble. He also offered advice for little Asuncion and studied her with his forced and awkward smile. He had to strengthen my dose of bromide; perhaps now I can get a little more sleep.

September 30th.

The final September! The time is approaching, the time is approaching. It is three o'clock in the afternoon, and I have calculated how many minutes remain until October twelfth: 8,460.

I could not sleep last night; the wind rose and the sea and the rain lashed. I lay and let time rush by. Thinking and brooding? Oh, no! Doctor Gudehus calls me a philosopher, but my mind is very weak, and I can only think: death, death!

October 2nd.

I am deeply overcome, and my emotion is mixed with a feeling of triumph. Sometimes when I thought of death, and people looked at me with doubt and concern, I noticed that they thought I was insane, and I would regard myself with suspicion. But no! I am not insane.

Today I read the story of that Emperor Frederick who,

it was prophesied, would die *sub flore*. So he avoided cities like Florence and Florentinum, but one day he did go to Florentium—and died. Why did he die?

A prophecy is insignificant in itself. The question is, will the prophecy take root in you? If it does, then it is already as good as proven, and will come true. So, is not a prophecy that arose and became strong inside me more valuable than one coming from the outside? And is the unshakable knowledge of the point in time at which one will die more doubtful than the knowledge of the place? Oh, man and death are unfailingly bound! You can pull death towards you with all your willpower and conviction, make it approach at the hour you believe in...

October 3rd.

Often when my thoughts spread out like the gray waters before me, seemingly infinite because they are shrouded in fog, I see something like the connectedness of things, and I believe I perceive the emptiness of ideas.

What is suicide? Voluntary death? But no one dies involuntarily. Giving up life, giving oneself to death invariably happens out of weakness, and this weakness is inevitably the result of an illness of the body or of the soul, or of both. One does not die before one has resigned oneself...

Have I resigned myself? I must have, for I believe I would go insane if I do *not* die on the twelfth of October...

Death

October 5th.

I think of it incessantly and it completely preoccupies me—I ponder over when and from where the knowledge came to me; I can not tell! At nineteen or twenty I knew that at forty I would have to die, and one day, when I asked myself insistently on what day it would happen, I also knew the date!

And now the day has come so near, so near that I can almost feel the cold breath of death.

October 7th.

The wind has become stronger, the sea is roaring, the rain is drumming on the roof. I did not sleep last night, but went down to the beach in my heavy coat and sat on a stone.

Behind me in darkness and rain stood the cliff with the gray house in which little Asuncion was asleep. My little Asuncion! And before me the sea tossed its dull foam up to my feet.

All night I looked out and thought to myself that this is how death or after-death must be: over there and out there an unending, dully foaming darkness. Will a thought of mine or a notion of me live and weave on, listening for ever to the incomprehensible tumult?

October 8th.

I will thank Death when he arrives, for the time will come so soon that I will no longer have to wait. Three short autumn days, and it will be over. I cannot wait for the final minute, the very last! Should it not be a moment of delight and inexpressible sweetness? A moment of the highest ecstasy?

Three short autumn days, and Death will enter my room—how will he behave? Will he treat me like a worm? Will he seize me by the throat and strangle me? Or will he plunge his hand into my brain? But I think of him as grand and beautiful, and of a wild majesty!

October 9th.

I said to Asuncion as she sat upon my knee: "What would you say if somehow I were soon to leave you? Would you be very sad?"

She lay her head on my chest and sobbed bitterly. My throat is choked with pain.

I also have a fever. My head is hot and I shiver with cold.

October 10th.

He came to me, last night he came to me! I did not
see him and did not hear him, and yet I spoke to him. It
is ridiculous, but he behaved like a dentist!

"I think it best if we get down to it right away," he
said. But I did not want to, and fought him off. Gruffly, I
sent him away.

"I think it best if we get down to it right away!" The
sound of it! It went right through me. So sober, so boring, so bourgeois! Never have I known a colder or more
scornful feeling of disappointment.

October 11th. (11 o'clock at night)

Do I understand? Oh! Believe me, I understand! An
hour and a half ago, as I sat in my room, old Franz came
in to me. He was trembling and sobbing.

"The young Miss!" he shouted. "The child! Come
quickly!" And I went quickly.

I did not cry; only a cold horror shook me. She lay in
her bed, her black hair framing her pale, tortured little
face. I knelt by her, thinking nothing, doing nothing. Dr.
Gudehus came.

"Heart failure," he said, and nodded as if he were
not surprised. This bungler, this idiot was acting as if he
had foreseen this!

I, however—did I understand? Oh, when I was left

alone with her, while outside the rain and the sea roared and the wind howled in the stovepipe, I slammed my hand down on the table: it was suddenly so clear! For twenty years I have been summoning death to the day that is to start in an hour, and in me, deep down, there was something that secretly knew that I could not leave this child. I would not have been able to die after midnight, and yet it had to be! I would have sent death away if he had come. But he went to the child first, because he had to obey my knowledge and my belief. Have I, myself, brought death to your little bed? Have I killed you, my little Asuncion? Oh, these are rough and poor words for such delicate and mysterious things!

Farewell! Farewell! It may be that out there I will again find a thought or sensation of you. Look, the minute hand is moving, and the lamp which lights up your sweet little face will soon be spent. I hold your small cold hand and wait. Any moment now he will approach me, and I will only nod and close my eyes when I hear him say:

"I think it best if we get down to it right away."..

Avenged (*Gerächt*)
"Study for a Novella"
1899

First printed in Simplicissimus, *August 4 and 11, 1899. First book publication:* Erzählungen, *Frankfurt, 1958. Written for* Simplicissimus, *"Avenged," like "Fallen," takes up the emancipation of woman, but from an odd point of view. The male protagonist's initial impression of Dunya Stegemann's physical unattractiveness give place to his desire for a sexual relationship. Dunya Stegemann, on the other hand, will have none of this; she does not reciprocate his ambivalent feelings. A free spirit, she seems to have gotten beyond the emotional problems the narrator is struggling with. This relationship closely prefigures the intimate yet oddly formal one between the liberated painter Lisabeta Ivanovna and the uptight writer Tonio Kröger in* Tonio Kröger.

"ON THE SIMPLEST and most fundamental truths," said Anselm late at night, "life will often waste its most original instances."

When I met Dunya Stegemann I was twenty years old and extremely foppish. Busy trying to sow my wild oats, I was far from done. My yearnings were boundless; without scruple I devoted myself to satisfying them, but along with the inquisitive depravity of my way of life I sought to combine in the most graceful possible manner an idealism that led me, for instance, to heartily desire a pure, spiritual—a *completely* spiritual—intimacy with a woman. Concerning Miss Stegemann, she was born of German parents in Moscow and grew up there, or somewhere in Russia. In command of three languages—Russian, French, and German—she had come to Germany as a governess. But, endowed with artistic instincts, she had dropped that career after a few years and was now living as an intelligent free woman, a philosopher and single, providing second- or third-rate newspapers with articles on literature and music.

When I met her on the day I arrived in the town of B., at the sparsely occupied table of a small boarding house, she was thirty years old, a large person with a flat chest, flat hips, light-greenish eyes incapable of looking confused, an extraordinarily fleshy nose, and a drab hairstyle of an indifferent blond. Her plain, dark brown dress was as bare of coquetry and decoration as her hands. I had never seen such unequivocal and resolute ugliness in a woman.

Over roast beef we got into a conversation about Wagner in general, and *Tristan* in particular. Her free spirit stunned me. Her emancipation was so involuntary, so without exaggeration and emphasis, so calm, assured, and natural, that I was amazed. The objective composure with which she wove expressions like "incorporeal lust" into our conversation unhinged me, as did her glances, her movements, the comradely way she laid her hand on my arm...

Our conversation was lively and profound, and after the meal, when the four or five other guests had long left the dining room, it went on for hours. At dinner we saw each other again; later we played on the out-of-tune piano, exchanged more thoughts and impressions, and understood each other to the core. I felt great satisfaction. Here was a woman with a totally manly mind. Her words went straight to the point, steering clear of personal coquetry, while her freedom from prejudice enabled that radical intimacy in the exchange of experiences, moods, and sensations which in those days was my passion. My longing was fulfilled: I had found a female companion with a sublime uninhibitedness that allowed nothing disquieting to rear its head, a companion with whom I could rest assured that nothing but my mind would be stirred; for the physical charm of this intellectual woman was that of a broom. Indeed, my confidence in this relationship only grew stronger, for as our spiritual intimacy increased, everything physical about Dunya Stegemann became more and more repellent to me, almost repulsive: A triumph of the spirit more dazzling than I could ever have longed for.

And yet...and yet: no matter how perfect our evolving friendship, and the innocence with which we visited each other in our apartments after we had left the boarding house, still there was often something between us, something that ought to have been utterly foreign to the lofty coldness of our idiosyncratic relationship....It always stood between us just when our souls were about to bare their last and most chaste secrets to each other, and our minds were working to solve their subtlest mysteries....An unpleasant impulse hung in the air, sullying it, making it hard for me to breathe....She seemed totally unaware of it. Her strength and freedom were so unfettered! But I felt it, and suffered.

So one evening, more sensitive to each other than ever, we were sitting in my room engaged in a psychological discussion. She had dined with me. Everything but the red wine, of which we were still partaking, had been cleared from the round table, and the completely unceremonious state in which we smoked our cigarettes was characteristic of our relationship: Dunya Stegemann sat upright at the table while I, facing in the same direction, was slumped down on the chaise longue. Our probing, dissecting, and totally frank discussion about the psychological state instigated by love in men and women took its course. But I was not at ease. I did not feel free and was perhaps unusually irritable, as I had drunk a great deal. That *something* was present…that vile impulse was in the air, sullying it in a way I found increasingly unbearable. An urge came over me as if to throw open a window, to banish this unfounded disturbing feeling immediately and forever into the realm of nothingness. What I decided to voice had to be dealt with, and was no stronger or more honest than many other things we had confided to each other. My God, she was the last person to be thankful for considerations of politeness and gallantry.

"Listen," I said, pulling up my knees and crossing one leg over the other. "There is one thing I keep forgetting to say. Do you know what gives our relationship its most original and delicate charm for me? It is the close intimacy of our minds, which has become indispensable to me, in contrast to the distinct aversion which I have for you physically."

Silence.

"Well, well," she said, "that's amusing." And with that my interjection was brushed aside, and we resumed our discussion about love. I breathed a sigh of relief. The window had opened. The clarity, purity, and certainty of the situation was restored, which, without doubt, she had needed also. We smoked and talked.

"Oh, and one thing," she said suddenly, "that needs to be brought up...you see, you don't know that I once had an affair."

I turned my head towards her and stared at her in amazement. She sat upright, very calm, and gently moved the hand in which she was holding her cigarette back and forth on the table. Her mouth had opened slightly, and her light-greenish eyes were staring fixedly straight ahead.

"You?" I exclaimed. "A Platonic relationship?"

"No, a...serious one."

"Where...when...with whom?"

"In Frankfurt, a year ago. He was a bank clerk, a young, very handsome man...I felt the need to tell you...I'm pleased that you know. Or have I fallen in your esteem?"

I laughed, stretched out on the chaise longue, and drummed my fingers on the wall beside me.

"Most likely!" I said with airy irony. I was no longer looking at her but kept my face turned to the wall, observing my drumming fingers. With one stroke the atmosphere that had only just been cleansed became so thick that blood rushed to my head and my eyes clouded.... This woman had let herself be loved. Her body had been embraced by a man. Without turning my face from the wall I let my fantasy undress this body, and found it repulsively appealing. I gulped down another glass of red wine—how many had I had? Silence.

"Yes," she repeated softly, "I am pleased that you

know." And the unmistakably meaningful tone in which she said this sent me into a despicable bout of shivering. There she sat, towards midnight, alone with me in my room, with a waiting, offering steadfastness, upright, motionless…My depraved instincts were in turmoil. The idea of the cunning that a shameless and diabolic digression with this woman would involve made my heart pound unbearably.

"Well," I said, my tongue heavy. "This is extremely interesting!…And this bank clerk, did he amuse you?"

She answered, "Yes, indeed."

"And," I continued, still not looking at her, "you would have nothing against having another such adventure?"

"Absolutely nothing—"

Abruptly, in a flash, I turned to her, propping my hand on the pillow, and asked with the impudence of violent craving:

"How about us?"

Slowly she turned her face towards me and looked at me in friendly astonishment.

"Oh my dear friend, whatever gave you that idea?— No, our relationship is too much of a purely intellectual nature…"

"Well yes, yes…but it would be something else! We could, regardless of our other friendship and completely apart from it, get together in a different way for a change…"

"But no! You heard me say no!" she answered with increasing astonishment.

I shouted with the rage of a rake not used to denying even his basest whims:

"Why not? Why not? Why are you acting so coy?" And I began moving towards her threateningly—Dunya Stegemann stood up.

"Pull yourself together!" she said. "Have you lost your mind? I know your weakness, but this is unworthy of you. I said no, and I told you that our sentiments for each other are of an exclusively intellectual nature. Don't you understand that? —I'm going now. It is getting late."

I was sobered and regained my composure.

"So I've been rejected?" I said, laughing. "Well, I hope this won't affect our friendship."

"Why shouldn't it?" she answered, giving me a comradely handshake, a rather mocking smile playing around her unlovely lips. Then she left.

I stood in the middle of the room with a vacant look on my face while I let this dearly cherished adventure run once more through my mind. Finally I clapped my hand to my brow and went to bed.

Anecdote (*Anekdote*)

1908

First printed in März (March), *Munich, 2:11, June 2, 1908. First book publication in* Erzählungen, *Frankfurt, 1958. Angela prefigures Felix Krull. She too is a spinner of illusions, female rather than male, who has the innate ability to oblige a world that is in love with its dreams and wants nothing so much as to be deceived. For Mann, the artist is a person shackled to the world of appearances, who performs for others a function both necessary for them and fatal to him. Mann's handling of this theme in this story is sophisticated: is the husband's denunciation of his wife the truth, or not? Is Angela, like Zola's Nana, in reality merely a crude person who happens to radiate sexual magnetism? Or is she really the radiant creature she appears to be?*

WE HAD EATEN dinner together, a circle of friends, and at a late hour were still sitting in our host's study. We were smoking, and our conversation was relaxed and even a little moving. We spoke of the Veil of Maya and its shimmering illusion; of what the Buddha calls "Thirst"; of the sweetness of longing and the bitterness of knowledge, of great temptation and great deception. The phrase "disgrace of longing" had been uttered; the philosophical principle was established: the goal of all longing was the overcoming of the world. And, stirred by these reflections, somebody told the following anecdote, assuring us that it had actually happened, exactly as he was telling it, in the elegant society of his native city.

"If you had known Angela, Doctor Becker's wife — heavenly little Angela Becker—if you had seen her laughing blue eyes, her sweet mouth, the exquisite dimples in her cheeks, the blond locks on her temples, you would have been enchanted by the captivating loveliness of her being, you would have been infatuated with her, as I and everyone else was! What is an ideal? Is it above all a life-giving power, a promise of happiness, a source of enthusiasm and strength, and consequently a sting and arousal of all spiritual energies by life itself? If so, then Angela Becker was the ideal of our circle, its star, its dream. At least I believe that no one, in the world she belonged to, could imagine her not being there without immediately experiencing a loss of the love of life and the will to live, without feeling a direct and powerful impairment. I swear this is how it was!

Ernst Becker had brought her from another town. He was a quiet, polite, and moreover a not particularly imposing man with a brown beard. Lord knows how he had managed to win Angela. In a word, she was his. Originally a barrister and public official, at thirty he had become a banker—apparently in order to offer a life of comfort and luxury to the girl he wished to bring home, for right after that he had married.

One of the directors of the bank, he had an income of thirty or thirty-five thousand marks, and the Beckers, who, by the way, were childless, were energetically involved in the town's social whirl. Angela was the queen of the season, the prize of the ball, the center of soirées. Her box at the theater was constantly filled during intermissions with people bowing, smiling, enchanted; her stall at charity fairs was besieged by shoppers rushing to lighten their wallets so they could kiss Angela's gentle hand, win a smile from her sweet lips. What would be the point of calling her sparkling or delightful? Her sweet attraction can only be portrayed through the effect it had on people. Old and young were transfixed. Women and girls worshiped her; youths sent her poems in bouquets of flowers. A lieutenant shot a senior civil servant in the shoulder during a duel sparked by a quarrel at a ball over a waltz with Angela. Later the two men became inseparable friends, bound by their adoration for her. Elderly gentlemen surrounded her after dinners, to reinvigorate themselves with her scintillating conversation and her exquisitely mischievous coquetries: blood rushed back into the cheeks of the old men, they clung to life, they were happy. Once, in the drawing room, a general had knelt before her—in jest of course, but not without giving full expression to his adoration.

And yet no one, man or woman, could really boast of being close to her, or being her friend, except of course Ernst Becker, but he was too quiet and modest, and also, no doubt, too phlegmatic to boast about how happy he was. There was always a good distance between us and her, and as circumstance would have it we seldom caught a glimpse of her outside the salon or the ballroom. If you actually thought about it, you realized that you never saw this splendid creature in the cold light of day but only in the evening, in the hours of artificial light and social warmth. We were all her admirers, but she had no friends—and that was fine, for what is the point of an ideal one is chummy with?

Angela apparently dedicated her days to the running of her household, to judge by the pleasant sparkle of her own soirées. These were celebrated, indeed the high point of the winter season, and, one must add, they were all her doing, for Becker was a polite but in no way scintillating host. At these evenings Angela outdid herself. After dinner she would sit at her harp, and with her silvery voice sing to the murmur of the plucked strings. It is not the sort of thing one forgets. The taste, grace, and vivacious wit with which she presided over the evenings were entrancing. The kindness that she radiated equitably among her guests won every heart, and the inwardly attentive, furtively tender way in which she would look at her husband showed us what happiness was, that happiness was possible, and filled us with a rejuvenating and aching belief in goodness, much as art bestows goodness in perfecting life.

That was Ernst Becker's wife, and we hoped that he appreciated what he had. No man in town was envied more than he, and, as you can imagine, he was constantly being told what a lucky man he was. Everyone told him so, and he acknowledged all these envious homages with friendly acquiescence. The Beckers had been married for ten years; he was forty and Angela around thirty. Then the following occurred:

The Beckers were hosting one of their exemplary evenings, a dinner of about twenty settings. The menu is exquisite, the mood most lively. Champagne is served with the sherbet, and a gentleman, a bachelor of mature years, rises to offer a toast. He praises the host and hostess, praises their hospitality, that true and bountiful hospitality that springs from an overabundance of happiness and the wish to share it with so many. The gentleman speaks of Angela, praises her from the bottom of his heart. 'Yes, my dear, wonderful, gracious lady,' he says, turning towards her with the glass in his hand. 'If I am spending my life as a confirmed bachelor it is because I never found a woman like you. Were I ever to marry, one thing is certain: my wife would have to be like you in every detail!' Then he turns to Ernst Becker and begs permission to tell him yet again what he has already so often heard: how much we all envy him, congratulate him, and wish him luck. Then the gentleman invites the other guests to join in his toast to our hosts, Herr and Frau Becker, whom heaven has so smiled upon.

The guests cheer and rise to clink glasses with the fortunate couple. Suddenly there is silence: Becker, Director Becker, rises, and he is deathly pale.

He is pale, only his eyes are red. In a shaken and solemn voice, he begins to speak.

For once—he stammers, inwardly struggling—for once he must speak. To finally free himself from the burden of truth, which he has borne for so long alone. To finally make us, dazzled and blinded fools, open our eyes to the truth about this idol, whom we have envied him so much for possessing. As the guests, some sitting, some standing, surround the glittering dinner table, wide-eyed, rigid, paralyzed, not believing their ears, Ernst Becker in a frightening outburst sketches the picture of his marriage—his *hellish* marriage.

How this woman—that one there!—is false, vicious, and brutishly cruel. How loveless and repulsively empty she is. How she lounges about all day in depraved and slovenly slackness, only to come to hypocritical life in the artificial light of evening. How all she does during the day is torture her cat in cruelly inventive ways. How she also tortures him to the bone with her malicious whims. How she has shamelessly betrayed him, cuckolded him with servants, workmen, with beggars who come to the door. How even before that she had pulled him down into the abysses of her depravity, humiliated, besmirched, and poisoned him. How he had borne it all, borne it for the love he used to have for this charlatan because she was really nothing but a miserable, pitiful wretch. How he had finally grown tired of everyone's envy, congratulations, and cheers; and now—now had to speak out.

'Why,' he shouts, 'she doesn't even wash herself! She's too lazy! She is dirty under those lacy frills!'

Two gentlemen led him out. The guests scattered. A few days later Becker, apparently following an agreement with his wife, entered a psychiatric hospital. But he was completely sound; he had just been pushed to the brink.

Later the Beckers moved to another city."

THOMAS MANN

Born in 1875, Thomas Mann lived in Munich from 1893, emigrating to Switzerland in 1933 and to the United States in 1939, returning to Zürich at the end of his life.

Mann's writing reveals many of the great artistic forces behind late nineteeth and early twentieth century Europe. His earliest works, including the novel *Buddenbrooks* (1901) and *Tonio Kröger* (1902), follow the model of Theodor Fontane in combining the European social novel with the most regional model of German literature. The thematic of the clash between burgher and artist, between the stolid philistine and the sensitive aesthete, is repeated in his famed novella of 1913, *Death in Venice*, and again in his great novel *The Magic Mountain* (1924). All these works explore, in part, the role of art and the individual in a workaday world, which has little patience or understanding of the aesthetics.

Other significant books include *Joseph and His Brothers* (1933–43), *Lotte in Wimar* (1939), *Doctor Faustus* (1947), *The Holy Sinner* (1951), and *Felix Krull* (1954). Mann was awarded the Nobel Prize for Literature in 1929.

SUN & MOON CLASSICS

SIGURD HOEL [Norway]
  The Road to the World's End 75 (1-55713-210-0, $13.95)

FANNY HOWE [USA]
  The Deep North 15 (1-55713-105-8, $9.95)
  Saving History 27 (1-55713-100-7, $12.95)

SUSAN HOWE [USA]
  The Europe of Trusts 7 (1-55713-009-4, $10.95)

LAURA (RIDING) JACKSON [USA]
  Lives of Wives 71 (1-55713-182-1, $12.95)

LEN JENKIN [USA]
  Dark Ride and Other Plays 22 (1-55713-073-6, $13.95)
  Careless Love 54 (1-55713-168-6, $9.95)

WILHELM JENSEN [Germany]
  Gradiva 38 (1-55713-139-2, $13.95)

JOHN JESURUN [USA]
  Everything that Rises Must Converge 116 (1-55713-053-1, $11.95)

JEFFREY M. JONES [USA]
  J. P. Morgan Saves the Nation 157 (1-55713-256-9, $9.95)
  Love Trouble 78 (1-55713-198-8, $9.95)

STEVE KATZ [USA]
  43 Fictions 18 (1-55713-069-8, $12.95)

THOMAS LA FARGE [USA]
  Terror of Earth 136 (1-55713-261-5, $11.95)

VALERY LARBAUD [France]
  Childish Things 19 (1-55713-119-8, $13.95)

OSMAN LINS [Brazil]
  Nine, Novena 104 (1-55713-229-1, $12.95)

JACKSON MAC LOW [USA]
  Barnesbook 127 (1-55713-235-6, $9.95)
  From Pearl Harbor Day to FDR's Birthday 126
    (0-940650-19-3, $10.95)
  Pieces O' Six 17 (1-55713-060-4, $11.95)

CLARENCE MAJOR [USA]
  Painted Turtle: Woman with Guitar (1-55713-085-x, $11.95)

WENDY WALKER [USA]
The Sea-Rabbit or, The Artist of Life 57 (1-55713-001-9, $12.95)
The Secret Service 20 (1-55713-084-1, $13.95)
Stories Out of Omarie 58 (1-55713-172-4, $12.95)

BARRETT WATTEN [USA]
Frame (1971–1991) 117 (1-55713-239-9, $13.95)

MAC WELLMAN [USA]
The Land Beyond the Forest: Dracula AND *Swoop* 112
(1-55713-228-3, $12.95)
Two Plays: A Murder of Crows AND *The Hyacinth Macaw* 62
(1-55713-197-X, $11.95)

JOHN WIENERS [USA]
707 Scott Street 106 (1-55713-252-6, $12.95)

ÉMILE ZOLA [France]
The Belly of Paris 70 (1-55713-066-3, $14.95)

*

Individuals order from:
Sun & Moon Press
6026 Wilshire Boulevard
Los Angeles, California 90036
213-857-1115

Libraries and Bookstores in the United States and Canada
should order from:
Consortium Book Sales & Distribution
1045 Westgate Drive, Suite 90
Saint Paul, Minnesota 55114-1065
800-283-3572
FAX 612-221-0124

Libraries and Bookstores in the United Kingdom and on the Continent
should order from:
Password Books Ltd.
23 New Mount Street
Manchester M4 4DE, ENGLAND
0161 953 4009
INTERNATIONAL +44 61 953-4009
0161 953 4090